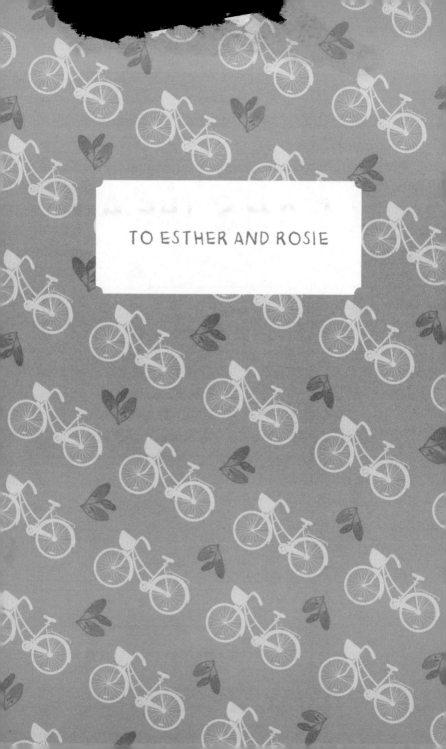

TO ESTHER AND ROSIE

HOPE JONES
CLEARS THE AIR

JOSH LACEY

ILLUSTRATED BY
BEATRIZ CASTRO

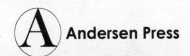

CLEAR
THE
AIR!

PLEASE SWITCH OFF
YOUR ENGINE I AM
TRYING TO BREATHE

First published in 2021 by
Andersen Press Limited
20 Vauxhall Bridge Road
London SW1V 2SA

Vijverlaan 48,
3062 HL Rotterdam, Nederland

www.andersenpress.co.uk

2 4 6 8 10 9 7 5 3 1

British Library Cataloguing in Publication Data available.

ISBN 978 1 83913 052 6

This book is printed on FSC accredited paper

Printed and bound in Great Britain by Clays Ltd, Elcograf S.p.A.

I'M GIVING UP
CARS TO
SAVE OUR
WORLD!

YOU'RE
DRIVING
US TO
EXTINCTION!

Hello.

Welcome to my blog.

My name is Hope Jones.

I am ten years old.

I am going to save the world.

'A man on foot, on horseback or on a bicycle will see more, feel more, enjoy more in one mile than the motorised tourists can in a hundred miles'

Edward Abbey

'There are no passengers on the Spaceship Earth. We are all crew'

Marshall McLuhan

'NO ONE CAN SING WHO HAS SMOG IN HIS THROAT'

DR SEUSS

'The bicycle is the most civilised conveyance known to man. Other forms of transport grow daily more nightmarish. Only the bicycle remains pure in heart'

IRIS MURDOCH

'Progress is impossible without change, and those who cannot change their minds cannot change anything'

George Bernard Shaw

'IF YOU WISH YOUR CHILDREN TO THINK DEEP THINGS, TO KNOW THE HOLIEST EMOTIONS, TAKE THEM TO THE WOODS AND HILLS, AND GIVE THEM THE FREEDOM OF THE MEADOWS'

RICHARD JEFFERIES

'THE PEOPLE HAVE A RIGHT TO CLEAN AIR'

PENNSYLVANIA CONSTITUTION

FRIDAY 30 MAY

Today I realised something very important. I have to stop pollution.

Why?

Because the air around here is so polluted that it almost killed one of my friends.

She couldn't breathe. I really thought she was going to die. It was so scary!

This week is half term, but we're not doing anything interesting because Mum and Dad both have to work, plus they're saving up for a holiday in the summer. I've been at Sports Camp every morning.

Some people love Sports Camp. My little brother Finn, for instance, can't think of a better way to spend a week than playing football, tennis, hockey, basketball, badminton and ping pong. I'd rather be at home reading a book, but unfortunately that wasn't an option. The only good thing about Sports Camp is my friend Selma being there too.

Today we had rounders, followed by a competition to see who could be the first to do fifty star-jumps. I had got to thirty-seven when I heard this weird wheezing crackling noise. I couldn't work out what it was. An animal? A bird? Something in the air?

Then I realised the noise was coming from Selma. She had stopped star-jumping and was standing very still, holding her chest.

I asked if she was ok. Selma managed to tell me not to worry, she just needed her inhaler. She put it to her mouth and took a puff, then another, but her breathing got even worse. I could hear her lungs croaking and hissing with every breath.

'It's the pollution,' Selma managed to say between gasps.

I wanted to know how to help.

'You don't have to do anything,' Selma said. 'Don't worry, I'm fine.'

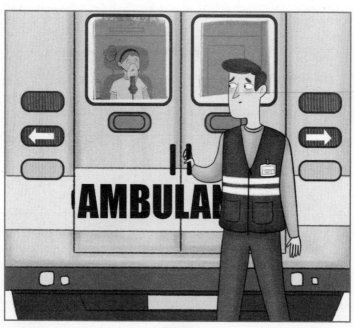

She didn't look fine. Her lips had turned blue.

She took more puffs from her inhaler, but they didn't make any difference.

I ran over to the coach as fast as I could and shouted, 'You need to help Selma! She's having an asthma attack.'

Selma still said she felt fine, but the coach asked me to get Callum, the first aider.

Callum was brilliant and knew exactly what to do. He rang 999, asked for an ambulance to come immediately, and said I could stay with Selma till the medics arrived.

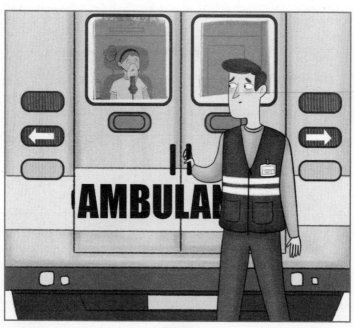

I wanted to go with Selma to hospital, but the paramedics said no, and sent me back to the group. I couldn't concentrate though because I was too worried about her.

Callum came over to reassure me that Selma was in good hands now and would be ok. He told me that asthma sufferers in the city have to be particularly careful in the summer as the pollution gets even worse. The local council has issued a high alert, which is why Selma has been told to carry her inhaler wherever she goes.

Sports Camp is only in the mornings, so Mum fetched me at lunchtime. We drove home, although I would have preferred to walk. I felt bad about being in a car, because our engine was pumping pollution into the air, poisoning other people's lungs and giving them asthma.

'Don't be silly,' Mum said. 'Selma didn't get asthma from *our* car. She got it from the thousands of cars and lorries around here, and the factories, and the boilers, and all the different things making pollution. You can't blame yourself.'

I told her that I don't blame myself; I blame pollution.

'You couldn't possibly stop pollution,' Mum said. 'It's everywhere!'

'I can try,' I said.

I've been saving the world for five months now. I gave up plastic for my New Year's resolution and started a protest outside our local supermarket. I became a flexitarian because I was concerned about the environmental impact of eating too much meat. I have been recycling and re-using as much as possible, and trying to persuade my family, friends and neighbours to do the same. From all this, I have learned one thing: doing something is always better than doing nothing.

✿ Hope Jones' Blog ✿

SATURDAY 31 MAY

I've got some good news and some bad news.

The good news: Selma is feeling much better today. Mrs Papagiannis (her mum) sent a message to my mum (Mrs Jones), saying she'll be back at school on Monday.

The bad news: pollution is a much bigger problem than I thought.

My friend Harry helped me do some research on the internet. I went round to his house for lunch.

His mum made wraps (hummus for me and chicken for Harry). They were dee-lish. Thanks, Mrs Murakami!

After lunch, Harry's parents wanted us to go in the garden, and enjoy the sunshine and fresh air, but Harry doesn't really like fresh air or sunshine. He prefers to stay indoors and use his computers.

He has six and three-quarters. The three-quarters is a computer that he's building from parts that he found on a skip and bought from eBay. It just looks like a pile of old rubbish to me, but Harry says once it's up and running, it will be powerful enough to search the universe for new planets. Don't ask me how.

Harry made a list of the main causes of air pollution:

```
Factories

Farms

Air travel

Burning fuel for heating or cooking

Pollen, volcanoes, dust blown
from the desert and other natural
phenomena

Road transport — cars, lorries,
etc — which cause air pollution not
only by burning fossil fuels in
their engines, but also from the
friction of their brakes and their
tyres on the road.
```

Of those six, according to Harry's research, road transport is by far the biggest cause of air pollution. If only we could remove vehicles from the roads in our towns and cities, the pollution would immediately get much better — and everyone would be able to breathe more easily.

Harry is brilliant with computers, so he can discover whatever you want to know. And things you'd rather not.

Like for instance: living in a city is the same as smoking an entire packet of cigarettes every day. YUCK!

Harry also discovered: around the world, air pollution kills seven million people every year; air pollution is linked not only to asthma, but also lung cancer, heart disease and diabetes.

Children are particularly vulnerable to air pollution because we breathe faster than adults, and our lungs are still growing. Pollution causes permanent damage to our bodies. If we breathe dirty air when we're kids, we will suffer the consequences for the rest of our lives.

Unfortunately, we can't *not* breathe dirty air, because humans have polluted our entire planet.

Only five per cent of the world's population now breathes clean air. Five per cent! In other words, one out of every twenty humans breathes clean air, while the rest of us – the other nineteen out of every twenty – breathe dirty air.

The only people who are breathing clean air are the ones lucky enough to live on top of a mountain or in the middle of nowhere, hundreds of miles from the nearest city.

I felt overwhelmed by all Harry's research, and quite depressed, but I did feel optimistic about one thing: I know we aren't breathing clean air, but we could be! If only we could get rid of all the factories, farms, planes, heaters, cookers, cars and trucks.

'How are you going to do all that?' Harry asked.

Good question! I wish I knew the answer.

'You'll find a way,' Harry said.

He's very nice. He always believes in me.

I hope he's right.

14

SUNDAY 1 JUNE

I wanted to spend today on the internet, researching ways to stop pollution, but Mum wouldn't let me.

'It's the weekend,' she said, 'so we're going to have some quality time with the whole family.' Which meant going to the park.

I didn't want to go to the park or have quality time with my family. I wanted to think about ways to save the world and make the air cleaner for Selma to breathe. But I'm just a kid, so I didn't get to choose.

On the way to the park, we were passed by an old car with great clouds of black smoke billowing from its exhaust.

'This is what I'm talking about,' I said.

'We all agree with you,' Dad said. 'We'd love the air to be cleaner round here. We just don't know what to do about it.'

When we got to the playground, Becca sat on a bench and played with her phone, Finn went on the zip wire, and Mum and Dad discussed how they might be able to cut down on our utility bills because we're spending too much at the moment.

I had some good suggestions. We could put solar panels on the roof and recycle our wastewater and replace our car with an electric one.

Dad said I wasn't being realistic, so I left them to their discussions and sat on the swings instead. The swings are a good place to have a serious think – and I had a lot to think about.

I was lost in my thoughts when Mum came and sat beside me.

'It's the weekend,' she said. 'Try to have some fun. You need to enjoy yourself.'

How can I enjoy myself when the world is such a mess?

Mum thinks I shouldn't spend so much time worrying about climate change and pollution and all the world's problems.

'I know you care about the future, Hope, and that's wonderful. It really is. Your father and I are so impressed by everything that you've achieved. But you can't tackle a huge issue like pollution, you simply can't, even politicians and scientists don't know what to do. You're brave and determined, but you're only ten, and you know what ten-year-olds should be doing on a lovely sunny day?

16

17

They should be messing around on the swings and the zip wire, not worrying so much about the state of the world.'

Mum's wrong about pollution. I can do something about it! I know I can. I just don't know what.

But she was right about one thing: I do love the zip wire.

MONDAY 2 JUNE

Today was my first day back at school after half term. Learning about pollution is much more important than my education, particularly on Mondays when we have PE all afternoon, but Mum wouldn't let me stay at home.

'You need to know how to read and write,' she said.

I pointed out that I can already read and write.

'You need to know how to do maths,' Mum said. 'So you can work out all the complicated sums about ecology and sea levels rising and how many years are left until we're all doomed.'

'Scientists do those sums,' I said. 'Not me.'

'You might be a scientist one day,' Mum said.

'I'd rather be prime minister.'

'You could be both.'

'Can you be a scientist and the prime minister?'

'I don't see why not, but you'd definitely need a good education. So, come on. We can finish this conversation on the way to school. Now can you please put your shoes on.'

School was actually all right. It was good to see my friends again.

Miss Brockenhurst went round the class and asked each of us what we had done over half term.

Harry had finished building his new computer and set it to search nearby galaxies for habitable planets.

Vivek had run 5K and achieved a new PB (Personal Best).

Jemima had flown to the Canary Islands and stayed in a hotel with a pool with amazing water slides.

Gwen had had her grandparents staying, so they went to Buckingham Palace and the London Eye.

When it was my turn, I didn't want to talk about Sports Camp because even thinking about it made me feel bored, so I told everyone about pollution instead, and explained that I want to clean up the air around here.

Jemima said she'd really noticed the pollution when she came back from the Canaries. 'It's so gross! The first few hours, you're wrinkling your nose at the smell and the grime. You can't believe it! But you soon forget about it. A day or two later, you've got used to it and don't even notice.'

Lots of people had ideas for tackling pollution.

Aaron recommended a car share. 'Then you'd only use your car half as much.'

I thought that was a pretty good idea.

Tom said we could easily make our own car more fuel efficient. 'Make sure the tyres are pumped up properly,' he said. 'Always drive with the windows shut.'

Gwen suggested I should try and persuade my parents to buy an electric car. 'Ours is really good,' she said. 'It does produce some pollution, but much less than a car with a diesel or petrol engine.'

Vivek asked if I knew about the pollution produced by boilers, stoves and open fires. Apparently, they cause even more pollution than cars. 'Check your heating system at home,' he advised me.

I'm feeling quite overwhelmed by so much advice and information.

Selma was back at school today, but she's not going to be here for long. Her parents have decided to move. They don't want to stay in this area any longer because the pollution is so bad.

I'm really going to miss her.

My best friend Zoe moved to Amsterdam a year ago. That was nothing to do with pollution, but losing my best friend was terrible. I don't want to lose another friend.

I said to Selma, 'Would you stay here if the pollution wasn't so bad?'

'Obviously,' she said. 'That's why we're leaving.'

'So if I stopped the pollution, you'd stay here?'

Selma laughed. 'Oh, Hope,' she said. 'You're amazing! You really think you can change the world!'

What's so funny about that?

♔ Hope Jones' Blog ♔

I've got a pollution solution.

I can't stop all the pollution in the world. I can't shut down the factories. I can't prevent lorries, vans, or other people's cars from driving around, sending smoke and fumes into the air. I can't even change the boiler in our house or buy an electric car (that's up to Mum and Dad, and they've promised to think about it). But I can do one small thing. I can boycott cars.

I'd rather do a girlcott, but that isn't even a word. Boycotts aren't named after boys, they're named after a man called Captain Charles Boycott.

Captain Charles Boycott

'Boycott'

Verb, noun

Meaning: A ban on a product or a company in protest against their policies or behaviour, usually for moral or political reasons. The purpose of a boycott is to raise awareness of an issue and to persuade the target to change their behaviour.

First recorded use: From the name of Captain Charles Boycott, an Irish landowner. In 1880, Captain Boycott tried to evict tenants from his land when they couldn't pay the rent. Locals responded by refusing to work for him. Local businesses would not trade with him. Even the local postman would not deliver his mail.

Throughout history, people have used boycotts to make a point and show their feelings. When slavery still existed, for instance, some people refused to buy products made by slaves. Mahatma Gandhi did a boycott of British goods because he wanted the British to go back home and let Indians rule their own country.

Many people boycotted South African wine and grapes to protest against apartheid and the imprisonment of Nelson Mandela.

Vegetarians and vegans boycott meat. I've been boycotting single-use plastic.

And from today, I am going to boycott cars.

My Clean Air Pledge

I am never going to drive in a car again.

Name: Hope Jones

Date: Tuesday 3 June

OFFICIAL LEGAL DOCUMENT

Signed **Hope Jones**

I asked the rest of my family if they would boycott cars like me. My little brother Finn said yes, definitely.

He's a hero, because he loves cars. When he grows up, he wants to be a footballer, but if Man Utd won't have him he would like to be a racing driver instead. Even so, he signed a copy of the contract and pinned it to his bedroom wall.

My sister Becca said could I please stop talking so much, because she was trying to concentrate, which really just meant she was doing something 'important' on her phone.

She thinks my boycott is stupid. She wants to get a car as soon as she's learned to drive. She says cars give you freedom and she can't wait to have one of her own so she can go and see her boyfriend Tariq whenever she wants, and her friends.

I had printed out another copy of the contract for Becca and I gave it to her to read when she wasn't so 'busy'.

I found it later in the recycling. Unsigned.

Mum didn't want to sign my pledge, although she promised to think about it, which usually means no.

'I love the idea of clean air,' Mum said, 'but we can't change the world on our own – or stop pollution.'

'You have to start somewhere,' I said. 'You're just one individual in a big world, but you can make a difference if you make your own small steps.'

Mum agreed with that, but she was still worried about giving up the car. 'A boycott seems a bit extreme,' she said. 'Couldn't we just drive a bit less? I don't think we can give up our car completely. What if we need to go shopping? What if we want to buy some furniture? We couldn't carry a table back from the shops.'

I didn't know the answers to any of her questions – but there must be a way to go shopping or buy furniture without producing pollution.

Dad got home late, because he had been stuck in a meeting that went on so long he lost the will to live. I asked him to join my boycott, but he said sorry, no, he couldn't, because to be honest he likes our car.

I was shocked. What does he like about a machine that pumps pollution into the atmosphere, poisoning my friend's lungs?

'Obviously I don't like the pollution,' Dad said. 'But I like driving around. I like being free to go where I want. I like being able to wake up on a Sunday morning and think, the sun's shining, let's jump in the car and go to the seaside!'

'When have we ever done that?' I asked.

Dad had to admit that he couldn't actually remember the last time that he had woken up in the morning, jumped out of bed, and done whatever he wanted. 'But I used to,' he said, 'in the DBC.'

That's one of his jokes – DBC means Days Before Children.

'Look on the bright side,' Dad said. 'We only have one car. Lots of families have two.'

Two cars! Why would anyone need two cars? We don't even need one!

Dad said, 'You need to remember something, Hope. We're already a very eco-friendly family. You stopped eating factory-farmed meat, and we pretty much have too. You stopped using single-use plastic, and we've mostly done that too. And we hardly use our car. We walk and cycle as much as we can. You shouldn't be so hard on yourself.'

'You don't have to boycott cars,' I said. 'But I'm going to, and so is Finn. You can carry on messing up the world as much as you want. But we're going to change things around here, whether you like it or not.'

WEDNESDAY 4 JUNE

I have been boycotting cars all day.

My boycott went perfectly this morning. The sun was shining and we had a nice walk to school.

The boycott went perfectly this afternoon too, because Becca picked us up from school and we all walked home together.

Boycotting cars is easy!

THURSDAY 5 JUNE

I had another brilliant boycott this morning. The sun was shining, and Mum walked to school with me and Finn, so we didn't produce any pollution.

Things weren't so good this afternoon.

'I can't get in that,' I said.

Mum told me not to be silly.

'I'm not being silly,' I said. 'I'm boycotting cars.'

'I know you are,' Mum said. 'Can you hop in, please? Finn's desperate for a pee. I don't know why he can't go at school, but he says he forgot.'

Obviously I couldn't get in the car. 'I'll walk home on my own,' I said.

Mum didn't like that idea any more than I liked the idea of driving home. She begged me to get in the car. Then she ordered me. She even tried to bribe me, offering me a pack of sweets in exchange for coming home by car. I was tempted, I really was, but I had to say no.

I don't know what would have happened if Gwen and her mum hadn't happened to be walking past. They stopped to say hello.

'This is so embarrassing,' Mum said. 'Hope is always doing crazy things like this.'

'It's not embarrassing,' Gwen's mum said. 'We've been inspired by Hope. My husband never used to see the point of recycling, but now he's become completely obsessive about it. We all think she's wonderful.'

'I think she's wonderful too,' Mum said. 'Sometimes I wish she could just be a bit more ordinary. Now, please, Hope, just get in the car, and let's go home.'

Obviously I said no.

Gwen's mum suggested a solution. 'We're walking home. We could easily go via your house and drop off Hope.'

Mum ummed and ahhed before finally agreeing. Before she drove off, she had one more question for me.

'How long is this boycott going to last?' Mum wanted to know.

'Until there's no more pollution,' I said.

'Oh, great,' Mum said. 'For ever, then.'

'Let's hope not,' I said.

Walking home was much better than driving. I got a chance to talk to Gwen and her mum, who have actually been thinking about selling their car and just using taxis, bikes and public transport instead. They do most of their shopping online already, so they don't need a car to go to the shops. They can take a train to visit their friends and relatives. Gwen's mum works at home and Gwen's dad cycles to his office, so neither of them needs a car for commuting.

'We'll rent a car if we ever need one,' Gwen's mum said. 'We'll save so much money, we can go on some amazing holidays instead. Maybe we'll go to Venice. You don't need a car there!'

FRIDAY 6 JUNE

Sometimes you have to suffer for your beliefs. Or at least get a bit wet.

It was raining so hard this morning that I was actually woken up by the drops rattling against my window.

'Do you really want to walk in this?' Mum asked. 'You'll catch a horrible cold.'

I don't mind a bit of rain, nor does Finn. And Mum should like walking with us – it gives her a chance to jog home again after she's dropped us off. She's always saying she wants to do more exercise.

Our next-door neighbour Mr Crabbe saw us leaving the house. He was just getting into his car.

'What a miserable day!' he called out to us. 'Do you want a lift? I'm going past your school.'

Obviously I said no.

'Suit yourself,' said Mr Crabbe, and he drove away in a big cloud of black smoke.

Only after he had gone did I realise that I hadn't even explained why we had turned down his offer, which made it all a bit pointless. He probably thought we just like getting wet. I'll have to go round tomorrow and tell him about my boycott. Unless he reads my blog? But I'm pretty sure he doesn't. He's never mentioned it.

We arrived at school soaked, but who cares? A bit of water never hurt anyone. And certainly didn't give them asthma, diabetes, heart disease, or lung cancer.

35

SATURDAY 7 JUNE

If you are boycotting cars, you have to make painful choices and difficult decisions. My little brother Finn had to make one this morning.

Finn has football on Saturdays. He didn't want to drive, obviously, but the pitch is so far away that you couldn't possibly get there on a bike. Unless you left an hour early, and they didn't.

'The game will have finished by the time we arrive,' Dad said. 'If you want to play, we'll have to drive. Or we can skip today's game. The choice is yours.'

Finn was desperate to play. He's the star striker and didn't want to let down the rest of his team. At the same time, he

didn't want to mess up the planet with any more emissions.

Dad was standing by the front door, jangling his keys.

'If we don't leave right now, we'll miss kick-off,' Dad said. 'Decision time.'

Finn looked desperate. The choice was driving him crazy. Football or boycott? Football or boycott? Football? Boycott? Football? Boycott?

'Why don't you drive?' I suggested. 'You could go on your bike next week, but you might as well drive today.'

'What about my clean air pledge?' Finn said. 'I only signed it this week!'

'You can have a day off,' I said. 'It's not the end of the world.'

Finn smiled for the first time all morning and rushed off to the car with Dad.

Did I do the right thing? Or the wrong thing? What do you think? Should I have made Finn feel so guilty that he missed his football? Or was I right about it not being the end of the world?

To be honest, I really don't know.

I wanted to ask Becca about all this, because she does philosophy and ethics at school, but she just told me to leave her alone.

'I'm not talking to you till I've woken up,' she said.

She was actually sitting at the kitchen table, drinking a cup of strong black coffee, but apparently that doesn't count as being awake if you're a grumpy teenager.

I went next door and told Mr Crabbe about my boycott, but he wasn't very interested. He thought I should have accepted his lift yesterday.

'I was driving past your school anyway,' he said. 'My car would have produced the same amount of pollution whether you came with me or not.'

That was a good point, and I couldn't actually think of a response. Maybe I should have got a lift with him. Even better, he should have left the car at home and walked with us. But he said he's never going to walk all the way to work.

I asked him why, even if he can't stop commuting, he needs such a big car. He lives alone. He doesn't have any children or pets. Why can't he get a smaller car which uses less fuel, produces fewer emissions, and won't make me cough so much?

'I love my car,' Mr Crabbe said. As if that was the answer to everything.

SUNDAY 8 JUNE

Today my boycott caused a big problem for my feet. I couldn't get any new shoes, which is annoying because my school shoes are full of holes and my trainers are too small.

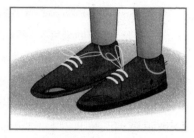

We had arranged to go on a family shopping expedition. Mum and Dad didn't want to walk or cycle because that would have taken hours, and apparently buses are too much hassle, so they insisted on driving. I suggested shopping online instead, but Mum says you can't buy shoes without trying them on.

'You can start your boycott again tomorrow,' Mum said. 'Come on, we don't have time for this. Let's go!'

Of course I said no.

Mum and Dad exchanged a look. I knew what that meant. They were going to pick me up and drag me to the car.

'Don't even try it,' I said.

'Please,' Mum said.

'No,' I said.

'We'll buy a tree,' Dad said.

'They don't sell trees in the shopping centre!'

Dad didn't mean that. 'There are schemes where you buy a tree to make up for your pollution. We'll buy one. We'll buy ten! Just get in the car.'

'It's not about trees,' I said. 'It's about the air round here.'

'We'll do something else about the air,' Mum said.

'Like what?'

They didn't have an answer to that.

In the end, Mum drove to the shops with Finn and Becca, while I stayed behind with Dad.

Finn wanted to stay with us and join my boycott, but Mum wouldn't let him because he needs new shoes too, plus some shorts and a jacket.

Becca didn't care about the pollution, because she's totally run out of clothes. That's what she says, anyway, although she's actually got so many that there's barely space in her bedroom for anything else.

When they had gone, Dad and I had cheese on toast together and read our books.

'Maybe your boycott isn't so bad after all,' Dad said.

Hope Jones' Blog

MONDAY 9 JUNE

My boycott is a waste of time.

That's what Selma says. She thinks I should have gone to the shopping centre by car, bought my new shoes and stopped worrying so much.

'You're just one person,' she said. 'You're not going to clean up the air round here on your own.'

'I'm not on my own,' I reminded her. 'My brother Finn has stopped using the car. I hope the rest of my family will too.'

Selma still thought we wouldn't make a big difference. 'Even if your whole family gives up driving, that's only one car,' she said. 'Think how many cars there are in the world. Think how much pollution they all make.'

'I'm not trying to change the whole world,' I pointed out. 'I just want to clean up our local area so you don't get asthma.'

'Think how many people live round here! Do you really think you can persuade them to give up their cars and walk or cycle instead?'

'Maybe,' I said.

'In your dreams,' Selma said.

Selma's family haven't decided where to move to yet. They just know that they don't want to live round here because the pollution is so terrible. I told Selma that pollution is bad everywhere, unless you're one of the five per cent of the population lucky enough to live on the top of a mountain or miles from anywhere, and Selma said her grandparents must be in that five per cent.

'They weren't before they retired,' she said. 'They used to live in Athens where the pollution is terrible – even worse than here! I got asthma every time I visited them. But now they've moved to an island, and the air is so clean and fresh, it's amazing. The sea breezes blow away all the pollution.

'Maybe we'll move to their island,' Selma said. 'Do you want to come and stay? We could go swimming in the sea every day.'

I'd love to visit Selma on the Greek island, but I'd much prefer her not to move away.

What if all my friends leave? I'll be so lonely and so miserable. And I won't be able to breathe.

I have to stop pollution!

Selma's right though, I can't do it alone. I'm just one very ordinary person and there is no way that I can clean up the air round here by myself. I need some help from other people.

Tonight I printed out thirty copies of my pledge. Tomorrow I'm going to take them to school and ask everyone in my class to join my boycott.

TUESDAY 10 JUNE

My shoes fell to pieces today when I put them on, so I wore my flip flops to school instead.

'Your teachers won't like that,' Becca pointed out.

Luckily Miss Brockenhurst didn't notice – even when she was right next to me. She must have been too interested in what I was saying.

I asked if I could describe the problems of air pollution.

'That sounds fascinating,' Miss Brockenhurst said. 'Could you just wait till everyone has finished their fractions?'

Three-quarters of two-fifths plus half of three-tenths equals waiting impatiently for everyone else to finish. Finally I got my chance to address the class. First I handed round the copies of my pledge, one for each person in the class, and one for Miss Brockenhurst. Then I described my boycott and explained why I never wanted to drive in a car again.

My Clean Air Pledge

I am never going to drive in a car again.

Name: _____

Date: _____

Signed

OFFICIAL LEGAL DOCUMENT

I had only just started explaining about the pollution produced by cars when Tom and Aaron started booing and complaining.

'Cars are beautiful,' Tom said.

'They're the best things ever invented,' Aaron added. 'Name one thing that's better!'

'Cheese,' said Selma.

'Trousers,' shouted Vivek.

Harry suggested the wheel.

I could think of a hundred inventions better than cars, but I didn't say a word till Miss Brockenhurst had quietened everyone down. Then I explained that I understand cars can be useful if you want to get from one place to another, and I appreciate they can be fun if you want to drive fast and feel the wind in your hair, but what about the smog in the city? What about Selma's asthma? Isn't that enough to make anyone hate cars?

Tom and Aaron didn't think so.

'When I grow up,' Tom said, 'I'm going to have a Porsche.'

'Porsches are rubbish,' said Aaron. 'I'm having a Ferrari.'

'You're crazy!' cried Tom. 'Everyone knows Porsches are way better than Ferraris!'

They probably would have carried on arguing all day if Miss Brockenhurst hadn't said, 'Thank you very much, Tom and Aaron. It's nice to hear how passionate you feel about your favourite cars. And thank you, Hope, for inspiring such an interesting discussion about pollution. Maybe we'll all be driving electric cars soon.'

Harry had something to say about that. 'Electric cars aren't as bad as conventional combustion engines, but they still produce pollution from their tyres, their brakes, and the dust on the roads, not to mention during the manufacturing process.'

'If we really want to stop pollution,' I added, 'we have to walk and cycle.'

During break, I asked Selma if she would sign my pledge.

She had some questions. 'But what if I need to go to hospital in an ambulance? I don't want to die because I'm boycotting vehicles.'

I told her not to worry. Like Finn and his football game on Saturday, sometimes you just have to jump in a car. It's not the end of the world.

Selma signed the pledge. She's happy to stop using cars as much as possible, particularly if that means she'll cure her asthma — and maybe even carry on living round here, rather than moving house.

I asked Harry to sign it, but he wasn't sure.

'Mum and Dad might not like it if I signed this,' he said. 'What if they want to drive me somewhere?'

'You tell them that you'd rather walk or cycle,' I said. 'You don't want to get asthma, do you? Or lung cancer, heart disease, or diabetes?'

'Obviously not,' Harry said.

He kept the pledge, although he hasn't actually signed it yet. He's going to discuss it with his parents. They care about the planet almost as much as me, so he's sure they'll want to do something about pollution.

There are two people who definitely aren't going to sign the pledge.

Yes, that's right. Tom and Aaron.

✿ Hope Jones' Blog ✿

WEDNESDAY 11 JUNE

A week! One whole week!

That's how long I have been boycotting cars.

I've been soaked to the skin a couple of times, and my shoes have fallen to pieces, but who cares?

I don't know what Miss Brockenhurst thinks of my flip flops – she still hasn't looked at my feet – but Harry is worried about me getting blisters, so during break he helped me research ways to get to the shoe shop without driving. Walking would be best, of course, but I can't walk that far in flip flops – and I won't have new shoes till I get to the shop!

'It's a paradox,' said Harry, who knows about these things.

I was concerned that buses and trains use fossil fuels and produce pollution, but Harry advised me not to worry.

'Buses aren't perfect,' he said. 'But they're much better than cars. They're mostly electric, and even the ones that burn fossil fuels are much more efficient than cars when you think about the number of people inside.'

Mum was delighted to hear we can get to the shoe shop by bus, but she wants to know how much longer my boycott is going to carry on.

'You can't boycott cars for ever,' she said. 'You'll have to drive in one eventually.'

You can imagine how I answered.

I can walk. I can cycle. Why do I ever need to go in a car again?

50

I want to breathe clean air, and if that means avoiding cars, then I don't mind.

'It's not that simple,' Mum said. 'What about going on holiday?'

'We can go on a cycling holiday,' I suggested. 'Or a sailing holiday.'

One summer we went dinghy sailing in Devon. It was brilliant! I'd be happy doing that every year – and we can easily get to Devon by train. We'd never have to use a car.

Mum had another question.

'We're going to see Granny and Grandad for lunch this weekend. It's my birthday, remember? You want to come, don't you? So you'll have to come in the car with us.'

'I'll walk,' I said.

'Don't be ridiculous,' Mum said.

'I could cycle.'

'It's much too far,' Mum said. 'You'd spend half the day getting there. When you finally arrived, you'd only have time to say hello, before you had to turn around and cycle home again. You'll have to come with us in the car.'

'I won't,' I said.

'Then you'll have to stay here on your own.'

'Fine,' I said, although I didn't really mean it. Of course I don't want to miss Mum's birthday. I've already bought her a brilliant present. I can't tell you what it is because she reads this blog, and I want it to be a surprise.

Somehow I have to get to Granny and Grandad's next Sunday for lunch. I just don't know how.

THURSDAY 12 JUNE

Miss Brockenhurst finally noticed my feet today – and she really didn't like my flip flops.

I had a question for her: 'What's more important, stopping air pollution or wearing the right shoes?'

'They're both important,' Miss Brockenhurst said. 'You can't come to school in flip flops.'

We ended up having a really interesting discussion about climate change and fossil fuels, which took up half the morning.

Miss Brockenhurst told us that coal and oil are formed from plants which have been buried underground for hundreds of millions of years.

When you burn fossil fuels, you release carbon into the atmosphere causing climate change and global warming. If we all stopped using fossil fuels, we could stop global warming.

Vivek had a question. 'Does that mean fossil fuels are made from dinosaurs?'

Some people laughed, but I didn't. I thought it was actually a very interesting question.

'I don't think so,' Miss Brockenhurst said. 'I'll have to look that up.'

Luckily Harry knew the answer. He knows almost everything about dinosaurs.

'Fossil fuels are mostly formed of plants which lived around three hundred million years ago,' he said. 'The first dinosaurs lived around two hundred and fifty million years ago. So you don't get any dinosaurs in coal or oil.'

'Thank you, Harry,' Miss Brockenhurst said.

I put my hand up.

'Yes, Hope?' Miss Brockenhurst said.

'The real dinosaurs are the fossil fuel companies,' I said. 'They're the ones who are going to be extinct soon. They should have changed to solar power and wind power and other renewable energy sources, but instead they carry on using fossil fuels, and destroying our planet. Fossil fuels should be banned!'

Miss Brockenhurst said, 'I can see that you feel very strongly about this—'

'I do!' I said.

'— so I suggest you do some research here in the school library or at home. Think about fossil fuels. How often do we use them? Look around your homes. What is powered by fossil fuels? How could we cut down on air pollution?'

When we stopped for lunch, Miss Brockenhurst thanked me for raising such interesting questions and starting such a fascinating discussion.

I said, 'Does that mean I can carry on wearing flip flops?'

'You can wear them tomorrow,' Miss Brockenhurst said. 'But if you don't have new shoes by Monday, I'll have to speak to your parents.'

Hope Jones' Blog

FRIDAY 13 JUNE

Today I went round my class asking who had signed my pledge.

Only three people said yes: Selma, Harry and Gwen.

Four out of thirty. Really? Can't we do better than that?

Obviously Tom and Aaron were never going to sign because they can't wait to start polluting the atmosphere with their Porsches and Ferraris, but I had hoped more of my friends would want to join the boycott. Unfortunately no one wants to stop using their cars.

'We have to drive to the athletics club,' Vivek said. 'There isn't any public transport.'

I suggested he could run there and back, but he didn't like that idea because he needs to keep his energy for the actual race.

'I couldn't stop using Dad's car,' Jemima said, 'but I could probably stop using Mum's. Would that count?'

Not really, I had to say.

Clementine said, 'I don't have to stop driving because we have an electric car.'

I reminded her that electric cars still produce pollution from their brakes and tyres.

I'm not giving up. Somehow I'll persuade them to change their minds.

I need to persuade my family too. Finn has signed my pledge, but Mum and Dad are still refusing, and Becca says not in a million years.

'Don't you care about the planet?' I asked her.

'Obviously I care about the planet,' Becca said. 'I also happen to care about my social life.'

Teenagers!

She wants Dad to drive her to a party tonight, then pay for a taxi to bring her back again.

I suggested she should walk or cycle, but apparently that simply isn't possible.

'Why don't you stay at home instead?' I suggested.

Apparently that isn't possible either, because we're super boring, and the party will be super brilliant, plus her boyfriend Tariq will be super disappointed if she's not there.

I pointed out that cars are super dangerous, but Becca says she is willing to take the risk if it means going to a great party.

SATURDAY 14 JUNE

Finn had football this morning. He didn't want to drive, so he and Dad both got up especially early, then cycled together to the pitch.

My little brother might be only seven years old, but he is definitely an eco-hero.

Becca stayed in bed, like she does every morning at the weekend, while Mum and I took the bus to the shoe shop. I told Cheryl (the owner) all about my boycott. She was very interested to hear about the air pollution problem in our area, but she says my boycott means I have to take especially good care of my feet.

'If you don't wear proper shoes, you'll damage your bones and joints, and cause terrible problems for your toes,' Cheryl said. 'Then you won't be able to walk, and you'll be in real trouble, won't you?'

Cheryl's right. If I'm going to be walking and cycling all the time, instead of driving, I need to look after my feet. Luckily my new shoes are really comfy.

On the way home, we stopped on the high street, and bought bread from Katya, veg from Mr Zaimoglu, and a chicken from Mitch the butcher. All the shopping filled four big bags – two each – so walking was exhausting. When we stopped for a rest, Mum said, 'I bet you wish we'd brought the car.'

'I really don't,' I said.

The biggest problem was all the pollution we inhaled from other people's cars.

Mum and I talked about her birthday, which is tomorrow.

'Please don't ruin my birthday,' Mum said.

Obviously I don't want to ruin her birthday, but at the same time I don't want to break my boycott by driving to Granny and Grandad's.

I don't know what to do.

I love birthdays, mine and other people's. I would never want to mess up anyone's birthday or stop them having the best day of the year. Tomorrow I have a simple and terrible choice:

EITHER be selfish and ruin Mum's birthday,

OR be selfish and mess up the planet.

What am I going to do? I keep asking myself that question. It's too far to walk or cycle. There isn't a train. I can't get from here to Granny and Grandad's without driving.

I can only see one solution: I'm really sorry, Mum, but I'm going to have to miss your birthday.

I feel miserable about my decision, and I know Mum won't be happy either, but sometimes you just have to do the right thing.

🚲 Hope Jones' Blog 🚲

SUNDAY 15 JUNE

First thing this morning, I got up and went into the garden in my PJs to gather some eggs, then I came inside and made a banner for Mum's birthday.

We had an amazing breakfast with freshly-squeezed orange juice, croissants and perfect scrambled eggs (thank you Henny, Penny and Jenny).

We gave our presents to Mum. She loved mine: a fitness tracker, so Mum can walk to and from school with me and Finn, and feel good about taking so many steps.

'You can test it out now,' I said. 'When we walk to Granny and Grandad's.'

Mum told me not to be silly. 'We're driving whether you like it or not.'

'I don't like it,' I said. 'You can drive, but I'll stay here.'

Dad pointed out that I wouldn't change the amount of pollution produced by our car, whether I drove in it or not. 'We're going to be driving there. We're using that fuel whatever happens. You might as well come with us.'

'I signed a pledge,' I explained. 'I made a promise. I can't break it. That would be wrong.'

Mum and Dad gave one another a look.

I wanted to know what that look meant. Did it mean: our daughter is so annoying! Or did it mean: we're going to pick her up and put her in the car whether she likes it or not! Or did it mean: of course Hope can stay here if she really wants to!

It didn't actually mean any of those things. What it meant was this: Mum took me aside and had a quiet word. She said, 'Today is my birthday and I want to have a nice day. I really don't want to argue with you, especially not today. So could you do something for me? Could you give me a special birthday present and agree to get in the car with the rest of the family, so we can go to Granny and Grandad's for lunch? I know you care passionately about your boycott, Hope, but could you have one day off? Just for me.'

I thought about Mahatma Gandhi, Emmeline Pankhurst, Nelson Mandela and Greta Thunberg, and tried to imagine what they would have done in this situation.

Then I thought about my mum.

And I knew what I had to do.

Driving in our car made me feel bad, but I would have felt much worse if I had ruined Mum's birthday.

Grandad already knew about my protest because he had been reading my blog. (Hello, Grandad!) He thinks I'm wasting my time.

'You'll never stop pollution,' he said. 'We'll just have to learn to live with it.'

I reminded him about Selma's asthma. She can't live with pollution, because it will kill her.

Grandad said, 'I'm very sorry about your friend. I wish things were different, but they aren't. The world is full of pollution. The streets are full of cars. You just have to accept that, Hope. You can't change it.'

Granny and Grandad don't just have one car. They have two!

I said, 'Why do you have two cars? You don't need two cars!'

'You're right,' Granny said. 'We hardly even need one car. We should probably get rid of them both. We can't afford them.'

Grandad laughed at the idea. 'What if I need to play golf and your grandmother wants to go shopping?'

I pointed out that they could walk, cycle, or get a taxi or a bus.

Grandad didn't like any of those ideas. 'Young people like yourselves might be able to go everywhere on foot or by bike, but us oldies can't. We need cars, or we couldn't get around. I'd never be able to see my grandchildren without a car. I know you care a lot about the planet, Hope, but you've picked the wrong target. Don't attack drivers.'

'I'm not attacking drivers,' I said. 'I'm only worried about cars.'

'I like my car,' Grandad said. 'I like being free to go where I want, when I want. You can't take that away from me!'

'What about my freedom to breathe?' I said. 'What about Selma's freedom to live here without getting asthma?'

'What about my freedom to have a nice peaceful Sunday without being shouted at by my granddaughter?' Grandad asked.

I think Grandad and I could have carried on arguing all day, and we probably would have done, if Granny hadn't called us to the table to have some lunch. Everything was delicious! Granny is the best cook in the world. She had made roast lamb (Mum's favourite lunch) and crispy roast potatoes (Mum's favourite vegetable). She even made a cheese soufflé especially for me, so I didn't have to eat the meat. I had never eaten a soufflé before, and it tasted almost exactly how it sounds: fluffy and French.

For pudding, Granny made an enormous thick creamy chocolate mousse, which has been Mum's favourite since she was even younger than me.

After all that, as if we weren't already so full that we might explode, we had a big sponge cake filled with strawberries and cream, and topped with lots of candles, which Mum blew out, followed by presents for Mum, then a family game of cricket in the garden.

I was so busy that I didn't even think about pollution again until I was sitting in our car on the way home, but I barely had time to feel guilty before I fell asleep. Soufflé, cake and cricket is a very tiring combination.

MONDAY 16 JUNE

Grandad is right. I'm not going to change the world by boycotting our car. I'm not going to clean up pollution by persuading my class to give up their cars. I need to ask more people to do something about pollution, which is why I am now asking YOU

to join my boycott and stop using your car.

You'll get fitter. The air will be cleaner. It's better for everyone.

I know you might need a car to get from one place to another. Perhaps your home is ten miles from your school or the nearest shop, so you couldn't do anything without driving around. But if you're like me, and you live in a town or a city, then I hope you'll say yes.

You can use my pledge if you like and print it out yourself. You just have to sign it and date it.

My Clean Air Pledge

I am never going to drive in a car again.

Name: _____

Date: _____

Signed

OFFICIAL LEGAL DOCUMENT

✿ Hope Jones' Blog ✿

TUESDAY 17 JUNE

Thank you, Tasha! Thank you, Bethany! I've never met either of you, but thank you for signing my pledge, and emailing me to say so.

If anyone else would like to boycott cars, please print off a copy and sign it yourself. You can email me to tell me all about it or ask me any questions. My address is:

hopejonessavestheworld@gmail.com.

Today I gave the pledge to our next-door neighbour Mr Crabbe. He was leaving for work at the same time that we were leaving for school. He read it quickly, then laughed, and handed it back.

'I don't think so,' he said. 'Not for me.'

'You could walk to work instead of driving,' I said. 'Then there wouldn't be so much pollution.'

'Just one problem with walking,' Mr Crabbe said. 'It would take me all day to get to work. See you later.'

WEDNESDAY 18 JUNE

One more person has signed my pledge!

I know only one person isn't going to make a huge difference, but I'm still pleased – and I'm especially pleased because this one person is my ex-best friend Zoe Madrigal.

If you're worried that she's my *ex*-best friend, you don't have to be. We didn't fall out or anything. She moved away and we haven't seen one another for a year.

This is what she said:

FROM Zoe Madrigal
TO Hope Jones
DATE Wednesday 18 June
SUBJECT Your pledge?
📎 **ATTACHMENTS** Me in Amsterdam

Hey Hope 😃

How are you? I'm pretty good. Although I miss you and everyone else at Durdle.

I love your blog! I've just signed your pledge, although TBH it won't make a big difference to my life, because we don't actually have a car!

I was really sorry to hear about Selma's asthma attacks. I'm going to message her too. I hope she's feeling better now. 😌

Anyway I loved what you said about plastic and meat, 😋 and I love what you're saying about pollution. I absolutely agree with you! I remember my old street. It was so gross and dirty and polluted. Things are much better here in Amsterdam. We don't even have to do a boycott because cars aren't allowed in the street where I live now, so the air is nice and clean, and you don't have to worry about being run over. Why don't you come and visit? You could see it for yourself.

Love ya!
Zoe

I wrote back to her immediately because I was fascinated to hear more about her street. It sounded so interesting. Why aren't cars allowed? How can it be so different to our streets here?

One minute later, Mum's phone rang. It was Zoe! We had so much to talk about, not just Selma and the asthma attack, and all her old friends from school and how much she misses everyone, but also she told me all about her new home in Amsterdam.

'Please come to visit me,' Zoe said. 'Things are really different here. Obviously I miss being back home. I miss you! But there are some things about Amsterdam which are much better. Like the bikes, for instance. You wouldn't have to do your boycott or your protest here, because there aren't any cars.'

I couldn't believe it. How could you have a city with no cars?

How does everyone get around? What happens if you need to go to the shops or visit your grandparents.

'Like I said, you should come and visit,' Zoe said. 'You can see everything for yourself.'

I wish I could.

When I'd finished chatting to Zoe, I asked Mum and Dad, who said maybe.

'We might be able to go next year,' Mum said.

Next year???

'We can't go any sooner,' Dad said. 'I don't get much holiday, and we don't have any spare cash at the moment.'

Talking to Zoe really made me miss her. I wish I could go and visit her. Even more, I wish she'd never moved away.

THURSDAY 19 JUNE

I'm an optimist. That's who I am. Dad always tells me that I am the glass half full type, and he is absolutely right. But I am not feeling so positive or optimistic today. In fact I was feeling so shaken and worried when I got home from school that I couldn't even write this blog. I had to sit down and talk to Mum for ages. Now it's late and I need to go to bed, but I just want to tell you about my miserable day.

Everything was normal for most of the day. School was fine, nothing special, same as always, until PE in the afternoon, when we did athletics in the playground. Mr Braithwaite divided us into teams and picked six captains.

Mr Braithwaite gave a baton to each captain and explained the rules of relay races. We spent a few minutes practising the handover, when you have to pass the baton to the next person at precisely the right moment, which is really quite difficult. Then he told us to get in our lines and blew a whistle to start the race.

I was in a team with Harry, Gwen, Selma, Tom and Vivek, who was obviously our captain because he's the best runner in our year, and probably the whole school. He went last, so he could win the final sprint, and he asked me to go first. I ran as fast as I could, but I was still only third by the time I handed it to Harry. He went, then Gwen did, and handed the baton to Selma. By this time we were in second place.

Selma sprinted round the playground at amazing speed. By the time she got back to us and handed the baton to Tom, we were only a couple of seconds behind the leaders.

All of us were cheering Tom, so we didn't immediately notice that Selma had sunk to the ground, clutching her chest. She was wheezing and gasping for breath. She took several puffs from her inhaler, but it didn't make any difference. I panicked. I thought she might die. Her lips had turned blue again.

Mr Braithwaite was brilliant. He stopped the race, picked up Selma and helped her inside to the nurse, who called an ambulance.

Selma is fine. Her mum put a message on the WhatsApp group to say it wasn't a bad attack and she'll be coming back to school on Monday. But I'm still very worried about what happened to her. I'm feeling very glass half empty.

FRIDAY 20 JUNE

I'm starving!

I didn't have lunch today because my school dinner gave Selma asthma.

That probably sounds crazy. How can you get asthma from lunch?

I'll tell you.

This morning, when Mum walked me and Finn to school, we found a big lorry parked on the double yellow lines by the front entrance.

I have seen that lorry before. I remember the driver unloading boxes and crates full of vegetables. But until this morning I had never noticed the black smoke gushing out of its exhaust.

I thought to myself: this machine has been filling Selma's lungs with pollution. Now it's doing the same to me and Finn. Someone needs to stop it.

I went up to the driver.

'Excuse me,' I said. 'Can you turn off your engine? It doesn't have to be running while you're delivering stuff to the kitchens.'

'I won't be a minute,' the driver said. Then he wheeled his trolley through the school's side entrance.

We waited for a minute, then another five, but he didn't come back.

'I've got to take you in,' Mum said. 'Otherwise you're going to be late.'

I felt so furious about the lorry!

Mum says I'm just worried about Selma, and that's probably true, but I'm also worried about all the pollution in the atmosphere.

When I walked up the stairs in our class, I looked out of the window and I could see that the lorry was *still* parked in the same place. The driver, Anthony, was unloading another trolley. The engine was still on, blowing more black smoke out of the exhaust.

I complained to Mr Khan.

I said, 'Do you know about the lorry which is murdering children from this school?'

He looked shocked and said, 'Which lorry?'

I explained about the lorry and its fumes that are filling our lungs with poison.

Mr Khan promised to ask the driver to switch off his engine while he was making his deliveries.

'He shouldn't use the engine at all,' I said. 'The pollution causes cancer and other diseases. And stunts the growth of our lungs. Children need to breathe clean air.'

I told him about my boycott.

'I hope you're not going to boycott lunch,' Mr Khan said.

'I'll have to,' I said. 'If it came in that lorry.'

Mr Khan said everyone needs lunch and I shouldn't even think about not eating it.

'We can't grow food in the playground,' he said. 'So our lunches have to get here somehow. At the moment, that means using lorries. But I hope we'll soon be able to use something else instead. Something greener.'

'I wish they could stop using lorries right now,' I said.

'I do too,' Mr Khan said. 'But I'm just a head teacher, not the prime minister.'

Mr Khan really is making an effort to turn Durdle Primary into the greenest school in the country. I've been helping him. The school has been cutting down on single-use plastics. We have vegan and vegetarian options for lunch every day, and the whole menu is veggie on Mondays, Tuesdays and Thursdays. He has even promised to talk to the school governors about putting solar panels on the roof, so the school could generate its own electricity. That's all great. But what about pollution? What about the lorry spewing out smoke right outside our school and killing us all?

Mr Khan said. 'Unfortunately, you can't change the world overnight.'

'Why not?' I said.

He smiled as if I had made a joke, then told me to get back to class.

Lunch was veggie lasagne, which I love. But I didn't eat it today, because I couldn't stop thinking about the lorry that had delivered the ingredients.

Hope Jones' Blog

SATURDAY 21 JUNE

I've got some amazing news. I'm going to Amsterdam!

Aunt Jess just read this over my shoulder and laughed.

'Hold your horses,' she said. 'The whole thing is dependent on finding some cheap tickets and a hotel. Not to mention asking your parents.'

You're probably wondering what's going on, so I'd better start at the beginning. Today Aunt Jess came to stay for the weekend. I love Aunt Jess, and I used to love her car too, but obviously I don't any more. In fact, I tried to persuade her to swap it for a bicycle.

'You must be joking,' Aunt Jess said. 'This car is the love of my life.'

Aunt Jess saved up for years to buy her car, and nothing makes her happier than nipping around town or driving through country lanes.

Aunt Jess has given Mum a very special birthday present: a night away in a hotel while she looks after us. Mum and Dad's hotel is in the middle of the countryside, miles away from anywhere, and unfortunately they're driving there in the car. I did suggest they should take their bikes on the train, but Mum said she wanted a weekend of relaxation and luxury, not punctures and rucksacks, so not this time.

When Mum and Dad had gone, the four of us made chocolate eclairs. Aunt Jess is an excellent cook and had brought the ingredients with her. Unfortunately the eclairs weren't vegan, because vegan chocolate eclairs are a physical impossibility. That's what Aunt Jess says, anyway, and apparently she is a world authority on the subject.

I felt sorry for vegans, because the chocolate eclairs were so delicious. I'm glad I'm a flexitarian. I ate three, and would have eaten a fourth if I hadn't felt sick and needed to lie down.

I asked Aunt Jess why she loved her car so much. 'Bikes are better,' I said. 'They're much healthier. You'd get fit. Your lungs would be cleaner. And you'd be saving the planet.'

'Please don't guilt trip me,' Aunt Jess said. 'Can't I have a few pleasures in my life?'

'You can have another chocolate eclair,' I said.

'I really shouldn't,' Aunt Jess said.

I told Aunt Jess about Selma's asthma attack and explained

the reasons behind my boycott. When I told her about Zoe's invitation, Aunt Jess perked up.

'Amsterdam is such fun!' she said. 'You'll have a brilliant time. It's always better to visit a city if you have friends there. They can show you all the cool places that normal tourists don't even know about.'

I would love to go to Amsterdam! There's just one problem. I'm only a kid. Mum and Dad won't let me go to the shops alone, so they'd never let me go to a foreign country. And even if they said yes, they're saving all their money for our summer holiday, and I couldn't possibly afford it myself, I've only got £11.21 saved up.

'Let's go together,' Aunt Jess said. 'How about next weekend?'

'I'll have to check my diary,' I said.

I was joking, because I thought she had been. But she wasn't.

'Seriously,' Aunt Jess said. 'You and I should go to Amsterdam for the weekend. Why not? I love Amsterdam. I'm sure we could find a cheap hotel. I would love to have a weekend away with my niece. What do you say? Shall we do it?'

Obviously I said yes. On one condition.

'I'm not driving there in your car,' I said.

'No problem. We can fly,' Aunt Jess said.

'I'm not flying either,' I said. 'That's even worse.'

Aunt Jess laughed. 'You are difficult! Fine, we'll take the train.'

Obviously walking or cycling would be better, but I don't think we could walk or cycle all the way from here to Amsterdam. So we're going to travel by train.

Zoe – if you're reading this – I'm coming to visit you!

Well, I might be, anyway. If Aunt Jess can find a cheap hotel and some cheap tickets. And, most importantly, if she can convince Mum and Dad to let me go.

SUNDAY 22 JUNE

I am actually going to Amsterdam.

I can't wait!

I'm so excited. I'm going to see Zoe again – and I'll find out all about the clean air and the empty streets and how the Dutch live without cars.

I literally can't wait!

Today I was worried Aunt Jess would have forgotten about the whole thing, but when she got up this morning, she made herself a cup of coffee and a piece of toast, then started searching on the internet. It took a little while, but she managed to find some train tickets and a nice cheap hotel for next weekend.

There was just one problem. Aunt Jess couldn't book the tickets or the hotel until she'd asked Mum and Dad's permission.

'Let's call them now,' I said.

Aunt Jess wanted to leave them in peace, but I felt too impatient, plus I knew they wouldn't mind, so we rang them.

To my surprise, they said yes, that sounds great. They were happy for me to spend a weekend in Amsterdam with Aunt Jess, as long as I promised to behave myself, and she did too. (That was Dad trying to be funny.)

I think Mum and Dad were just in a good mood because they are having such a wonderful weekend away.

Finn and Becca both think it's very unfair.

'Why does *she* get to go to Amsterdam?' Becca complained to Mum and Dad when they got back. 'I've always wanted to go there.'

'You can go one day,' Mum replied. 'We all get different opportunities in life. This is Hope's chance to have a weekend away with her aunt and see her best friend. You'll have your own chance soon enough.'

I can't wait! (Did I say that already?)

MONDAY 23 JUNE

Selma came back to school today. I wish she hadn't because her asthma is only going to get worse. Our neighbourhood isn't safe for her.

If you're wondering why, the answer is very simple.

When Mum picked us up at the end of the day, there were lots of cars parked outside our school with their engines running. Pumping foul gases into the air. Poisoning us all.

How many times have I walked past them before?

Hundreds. Literally.

But today was the first day that I really saw them. I must have been especially sensitive because I was thinking about Selma's asthma attack. Maybe I was thinking about Anthony's lorry too.

Anyway, I stopped, and counted up the cars. There were ten, and six of them had their engines switched on, although they weren't going to be moving any time soon because the drivers were still waiting for their kids to come out of the school.

I walked along the line of cars, asking each of those six drivers to turn off their engines.

The woman in the first car said, 'Yes, of course. Thanks for pointing it out.'

I thanked her and moved on.

'I wish I could help,' said the man in the second car. 'But I'm charging my phone.'

I'm sure you don't need the engine running to charge your phone!

But he refused to turn it off.

The drivers of the third, fourth and fifth cars agreed to switch off their engines, which was very nice of them. One of them promised that she'd always turn off her engine from now on. Another admitted she'd never thought about the pollution she was producing.

The woman in the sixth car wasn't so friendly. First she pretended not to see or hear me, then she claimed she couldn't possibly turn off her engine because of the heat.

'I'm keeping cool,' she said. 'I need the air con.'

My mouth dropped open. I couldn't believe what I had heard.

'Why don't you just open the window?'

'Because I prefer the air con,' she said. 'It feels fresher.'

What? That doesn't make sense! How can air con feel fresher than fresh air?

She said, 'The air around here is so polluted.'

'Yes! By people like you! If you switched off your engine, the air would be fresher – and you wouldn't need your air con!'

'There's no point arguing,' Mum said.

Of course there is! Those cars are pumping out poisonous gases right outside my school. I've got to argue with them! And arguing works – I persuaded four out of six to turn off their engines.

But Mum wouldn't let me argue more. She dragged me away, saying she didn't want to make a scene in front of all the other parents.

I felt so furious! It took me ages to calm down. I was still feeling cross when we got home. Becca says anger is a useful emotion and you need to channel it into action, which sounds like a very good idea. The only question is: how? I thought and I thought and I thought, and finally I came up with a brilliant idea.

I don't have any power or money. There's only one thing I can do: I can tell people what I think.

So that's what I'm going to do. If they know about the pollution problem, they'll stop driving their cars. I just have to tell them.

So I made a big sign.

TUESDAY 24 JUNE

Today I took my sign to school.

I don't know if my protest made much difference. A couple of drivers beeped their horns, and some others waved, but most of them just stopped and dropped off their kids outside the school without taking any notice of me, let alone switching off their engines.

Mr Khan came to see what I was doing. I asked him to have a word with all the idling drivers who refused to switch off their car engines.

'Unfortunately I can't,' Mr Khan said. 'They're not on school property. They're in the street, so they can do what they want. It's a free country.'

'You mean they're free to poison us?' I said.

Mr Khan didn't answer that, because he was already hurrying away to remind Olivia's mum that dogs have to be tied up outside the gates, not brought into the playground.

I talked to Jemima Higginbotham's dad. He was dropping off Jemima on the double yellow lines outside the school. I asked him to turn off his engine while he and Jemima chatted about who was picking her up later, but he refused.

'You need to relax,' he said. 'I'm only stopping here for a second.'

I explained about the poisonous pollution caused by idling engines, but he wasn't interested. He didn't even seem to care, and he actually interrupted me in mid-sentence, saying, 'If you stopped talking so much, I might be able to arrange things with my daughter, then I could leave, and my engine wouldn't be causing you any problems. We'd all be happy!'

Mr Higginbotham might not care, but my friend Harry thinks I'm absolutely right about pollution. He has promised to come and join my protest tomorrow. So has Finn.

Together we're going to clean up the world.

One car at a time.

WEDNESDAY 25 JUNE

This morning Harry, Finn and I protested outside the school.

To be honest it didn't go particularly well. No one took much notice of us.

I felt furious with the drivers. Why can't they turn off their engines? Even better, why can't they leave their cars at home?

By standing here, doing my protest, trying to make the world a better place, I am being poisoned even more. I'm breathing in great gulps of toxic gases which are murdering my lungs. But I'm not going to give up.

I talked to Anthony, the lorry driver who delivers our school lunches, he wasn't very happy to see me.

'I'm only doing my job,' he said.

'You're poisoning us,' I said. 'Is that your job?'

Anthony climbed into his cab and turned off the engine.

'Happy now?' he said.

'Happier,' I said. 'But I'd be even happier if you could get rid of this horrible old lorry and use an electric engine instead, so you weren't polluting the air around our school.'

Anthony promised to take it up with his manager.

Harry and I made another banner in art class and protested with it after school. I think it's a big improvement.

I didn't just show my banner to the drivers in the cars. I also talked to anyone who walked past, telling them the truth about air pollution.

You would have thought everyone knew the facts already, but they don't. It's amazing how little they know!

I had a long conversation with Mrs Ribblethwaite. She was fascinated to hear about air pollution. She said, 'So that's why I'm coughing all the time!'

'We are all being poisoned,' I said. 'Pollution is making us ill. And making our lives shorter. We have to stop using petrol and diesel. We have to give up our cars.'

'We don't have a car any more,' Mrs Ribblethwaite said. 'Not since Terry had his accident.'

I told her that she's lucky, because the pollution is actually worse inside a car than outside. Motorists breathe in even more harmful gases than cyclists or joggers.

A car is like a box full of poison.

The driver and the passengers are trapped in the box, taking in great gulps of poison with every breath, messing up their blood, their brains, their lungs, their insides.

If you want to live a long and happy life, you need to get out of that poison box!

🚲 Hope Jones' Blog 🚲

THURSDAY 26 JUNE

Harry has done some research for me. He found a site which calculates how much pollution is produced by different forms of transport, and he made a little chart to show the difference between flying to Amsterdam, driving there, or travelling by train.

London to Amsterdam:
train, car, or plane, which is better?

A comparison of the pollution produced by one person when they travel by train, car, or plane. This has been made by Harry Murakami for his friend Hope Jones.

	TRAIN 🚆	CAR 🚗	PLANE ✈️
Carbon dioxide (causes climate change)	32.8 kg	100.4 kg	149.4 kg
Particulate matter (causes air pollution)	9.2 g	9.8 g	21.6 g
Nitrogen oxide (also causes air pollution)	73.4 g	416.8 g	1014.8 g

IMPORTANT INFORMATION: These are return journeys i.e. London to Amsterdam, then Amsterdam to London.

MORE IMPORTANT INFORMATION: I calculated these amounts on a really good website **http://www.ecopassenger.org/**

99

Thanks, Harry! This information is so interesting, and very useful. Now I know exactly how much better train travel is than plane travel.

We walked back from school with Mrs Ahmed, who was picking up Mo and Joe. All three of them were really interested to learn about air pollution.

I explained that pollution is terrible for everyone, but it's worst for old people and young people.

Babies in buggies inhale very high levels of pollution because they are closer to the exhaust pipes of cars and lorries.

Schoolchildren breathe polluted air on the school run and in our playgrounds, which are often built beside main roads.

How crazy is that? Don't you think schools should be built as far away as possible from poisonous cars and lorries?

It's disgusting and unfair. I want clean air.

Mrs Ahmed agreed with me about everything.

She said there's just one problem: 'I don't have time to do anything about it.'

'You could join my protest,' I said. 'You're very welcome to come and stand here with me. You could make your own banner or borrow one of mine.'

Mrs Ahmed shook her head. 'I'd love to,' she said, 'but I've got to get these kids home and make their tea.'

According to Mrs Ahmed, she and all the other adults are too busy worrying about their mortgages and their jobs and what to cook for tea, so they don't have time to worry about things like pollution. They just don't have enough time or space in their brain to think about the planet.

'I wish things were different, but that's how life is,' she said. 'I'm rushed off my feet all the time.'

I don't have a job or a mortgage, so I've got time to protest. I want to tell these drivers what I think of them and their cars.

They are killing me.

They are killing themselves.

And they're killing you too.

(Unless you live on top of a mountain, miles from anywhere.)

Hope Jones' Blog

FRIDAY 27 JUNE

Guess where I am?

We've only been in Amsterdam a few hours, and we've already seen three canals, a hundred tulips, and about a million bicycles.

We haven't seen Zoe yet. We're going to meet up with her first thing tomorrow, but we're here in her city – and it's brilliant. I can see why she likes living here.

This afternoon, when I came out of school, Aunt Jess was waiting at the gates to pick me up. Mum was there too, collecting Finn. Mum gave me a big hug, told me to look after myself and handed over my bag and my passport.

Together, Aunt Jess and I took a train to the centre of London. We arrived at St Pancras International, passed through passport control and got on the Eurostar.

The Eurostar was much better than a plane: quick, easy and, of course, environmentally friendly. I brought a copy of Harry's calculations to show Aunt Jess, who was very impressed.

Amsterdam Central Station is right in the middle of the city, so we could walk straight to our hotel. There was just time to have a pizza in a restaurant, then collapse on the beds in our room. International travel is exhausting, and we've got a busy day tomorrow, so goodnight!

SATURDAY 28 JUNE

Wow.

Amsterdam is amazing.

We're only staying here for a couple of days, but you can do a lot in two days. Especially when you have Zoe, her mum and her stepdad to show you around.

Zoe's stepdad, Alexander, is Dutch, which is why they came to live here. Zoe and her mum only moved a year ago, but they already know their way around the city, and Zoe can already speak excellent Dutch. I can't imagine moving to a country where you can't speak a single word of their language, but Zoe says it has actually been fun, and not too difficult. She had to learn quickly, or she wouldn't have known what was going on at school.

They picked us up from our hotel and took us straight to Anne Frank's house.

You probably know about Anne Frank already. If you don't, then I'll just tell you that she was a Jewish girl who wrote a diary about her life. She was born in Germany in 1929, and moved to Amsterdam with her family when she was four. The Germans invaded the Netherlands in 1940. The Nazis started rounding up Jewish people to send them to work camps. Mr and Mrs Frank hid themselves and their children, Anne and her sister, in some rooms at the top of a house, with the entrance hidden behind a bookcase. There they stayed for the next two and a half years. They had to be completely secret, creeping around, never making any noise, always scared that they were going to be betrayed or seen by the Nazis.

Eventually their hiding-place was discovered by the police. Anne was taken to a concentration camp, where she died in February 1945, only three months before the end of the war.

Her house is the saddest place I have ever been.

When Anne died, she was only fifteen. Even younger than my sister Becca.

Aunt Jess bought me a copy of Anne Frank's diary. I'm going to start reading it on the train home. I'd like to read it now, but I know it's going to make me cry and I don't want to feel sad while I'm in Amsterdam.

'Put it out of your mind for now,' Zoe's mum said. 'I think if Anne Frank was still alive today, she would tell you to forget about the Nazis and that whole horrible period of our history and enjoy your weekend in Amsterdam.'

So that's what I did.

We went to a tulip museum, which really was a museum about tulips. It was actually quite interesting. Then we walked along the canals to an amazing art gallery and a beautiful old church. We stopped for lunch in a nice café and ate delicious sandwiches.

There was so much more to see – we could have spent the whole day visiting museums and wandering along the canals, looking at beautiful houses – but Zoe's stepdad said it was time to take a bus to a different part of the city.

'You have seen the sights for tourists,' Alexander said. (He has the best accent! I wish I could write it down.) 'Now we will see a sight which is not for tourists. This is only for people who live in Amsterdam.'

The bus took us to the neighbourhood where Zoe and her family have lived ever since they moved here. Their street isn't famous.

No one would come here on a guided tour. We were the only tourists. But I think it was one of the best things I have ever seen.

Here are two pictures of their street.

The first photo is from ten years ago.

We took the second one today.

Spot the difference!

Ten years ago, this street was full of cars. The air was polluted. Parking spaces lined the pavements, so you could barely find enough space to walk to your own home.

Now the street is entirely different. You can walk up and down without worrying about being run over. You can stop to smell the herbs growing in window boxes. You can sit down and have a drink in the café or chat to your friends outside their house.

Halfway down the street is a school. Parents can't take their children to school by car, because cars aren't allowed to park anywhere near the school's entrance. Instead, everyone has to walk or cycle. Even the air inside the playground is cleaner than the rest of the city because a green wall has been planted around the school, protecting the pupils from pollution.

If Zoe, her mum, or her stepdad are ever feeling worried about air pollution, or curious, they can check the readings on a monitor at the end of the street, which tells you exactly how much poisonous gas is currently in the atmosphere – and how much more you would be inhaling if you were walking down one of the main roads in Amsterdam, just a mile away.

This street has been transformed from a smog-filled, air-polluting, climate-changing, global-warming nightmare to a happy haven of clean air and environmental friendliness.

No one is poisoned by pollution.

It was very inspiring. I want to live in a street like this. I want to go to a school like this. I want to breathe clean air.

Aunt Jess was inspired too.

'I love this place,' she said. 'It makes me want to move.'

'Amsterdam is wonderful,' Zoe's mum said. 'You should come and live here for a few months. See if you like it.'

'You'd have to sell your car and buy a bike,' I pointed out.

Aunt Jess nodded. 'That might be good too.'

I couldn't believe it. 'You love that car!'

'I do,' Aunt Jess agreed. 'But that doesn't mean I shouldn't change things. You know how it is, Hope, sometimes you love someone, but you know he's not good for you. A car can be just the same.'

We visited Zoe's apartment, then had dinner in her favourite restaurant, which is just around the corner. I was a bit nervous because I had never eaten Moroccan food before, but Zoe promised I would love it – and she was right! Wow, Moroccan food is so tasty. Zoe said the most famous Moroccan speciality is a special pie baked full of pigeons, but I didn't want to try that. Instead I had carrot salad and a special stew called a tagine and the nicest bread I have ever tasted. It was so yummy!

Today has been amazing, but now I'm exhausted.

Goede nacht, slaap lekker.

(Zoe taught me the Dutch for: 'Goodnight, sleep well'.)

✿ Hope Jones' Blog ✿

SUNDAY 29 JUNE

Goedemorgen!

(That's 'Good morning' in Dutch.)

Usually Aunt Jess has a long lie-in on Sundays, but this morning we both got up bright and early because we wanted to explore as much as possible before it was time to get our train home. We checked out of our hotel straight after breakfast and walked to the train station, where we left our luggage in some lockers, then rented two bikes. We cycled along the canal to the Van Gogh museum.

There are cycle lanes everywhere in Amsterdam, so cycling is very safe. Not like at home where you can't cycle anywhere because you're too worried that you'll be knocked off your bike by a bus.

I usually think museums are quite boring, but the ones in Amsterdam are different. Yesterday I really liked learning about Anne Frank and tulips. Today I loved seeing Van Gogh's pictures. They are so great!

I bought a poster for me and some postcards for Becca and the rest of my family.

We cycled back to the centre of the city, returned our bikes, then met Zoe, her mum and her stepdad, who took us to one of their favourite cafés for lunch. We had a delicious lunch of toasted cheese sandwiches and chips.

When I'm older, I want to live in Amsterdam. It's the best city in the world.

Zoe's stepdad looked at the time. 'You have only a few minutes before you have to go to the train station. Do you want to try one more Dutch speciality?'

I felt so sad saying goodbye to Zoe. Seeing her made me remember why we were best friends. Obviously I have great friends now (hi, everyone!), but I do really miss Zoe.

I hope I'll see her again soon.

MONDAY 30 JUNE

Home sweet home.

Travelling is fun, but coming home is nice too.

I wonder if Henny, Penny and Jenny missed me while I was away?

I don't think they even noticed I was gone. Dad says they've been laying lots of eggs, so they must have been happy.

I missed them. I missed Mum and Dad too. I didn't exactly miss Finn or Becca, but it was quite nice to see them again.

I can't stop thinking about Zoe's neighbourhood. Her home is surrounded by trees and flowers. The kids at her local school don't cough and choke all the time, because they aren't being poisoned with every breath.

There's no chance of us actually moving to Amsterdam because Mum and Dad don't want to, so I'll have to move Amsterdam here instead.

I don't mean that literally. I couldn't dig any canals, let alone afford all those Van Goghs. But we could make some changes to our neighbourhood and my school, and make them more like Zoe's.

Hope Jones' Blog

I took my plan to school today and showed it to Mr Khan. I explained that I had been inspired by visiting Amsterdam. He was very interested to hear about my weekend away.

'I haven't been to Amsterdam since I was a student,' he said. 'Did you go to the Van Gogh museum?'

'I did,' I said. 'And Anne Frank's house. But I saw something else very interesting too – something that most tourists don't ever get to see.'

Mr Khan was really interested to hear about Zoe and where she's living now. I showed him some pictures of her neighbourhood. Then I gave him my plan.

Suggestions for improving the air quality in our school.

By Hope Jones

1: Install air filters in every classroom.

2: Plant a green wall around the playground, full of plants which will soak up pollution, and stop us from being poisoned by all the cars and lorries in the streets around the school.

3: Pedestrianise the streets around the school, so there is no pollution. Parents and staff have to walk or cycle to school. No cars!

'This is wonderful,' Mr Khan said. 'I'm so impressed by all your ideas, I would love to implement them.'

'Great,' I said. 'When are you going to start?'

'I'm very sorry,' Mr Khan said. 'We simply don't have a budget for things like air filters or a green wall. We barely have enough for basics like pencils, paper and books for the school library.'

I would have liked to help, but I spent all my pocket money in Amsterdam.

'What about banning cars from the streets outside the school?' I asked.

Mr Khan shook his head. 'I can't help with that. The streets aren't my responsibility. You'd have to talk to the council.'

I was very disappointed. 'So you can't do anything? You just want us to breathe polluted air?'

'I'm sorry, Hope. I wish I could be more positive. Of course I'll do what I can to help. I shall certainly bring this up at my next meeting with the governors.'

'When will that be?'

'We're not meeting again till nearer the end of term. But I promise I will discuss your proposals with them then.'

I couldn't believe it. 'Near the end of term! That's not for years!'

'It's only a few weeks away,' Mr Khan said. 'You'll just have to be patient.'

I felt so cross. 'Don't you care that we're breathing bad air?'

'Of course I care,' Mr Khan said. 'I'd help if I could. You know I want to make this school as green as possible. But I can't change the world.'

'You could if you really wanted to,' I said.

I asked Mr Khan how he got to school. He confessed that he had come by car, but he did remind me that the school already does something about air pollution.

He said, 'Once a year, in October, we encourage everyone to walk to school for a week. Maybe you could devote your energy to that instead? You could arrange some fundraising around Walk to School Week.'

I said, 'Once a year? What's the point of that? You should be persuading people to walk to and from school twice a day, not once a year!'

'The world isn't perfect, but we're doing what we can,' Mr Khan said. 'Every little helps.'

I cannot wait till October. That's not for three months! We need to change things right now.

WEDNESDAY 2 JULY

Four weeks!

That's how long I have been boycotting cars.

I've been in the car to go to Granny and Grandad's, and again driving back, but that's all. Only two car journeys in four weeks – that's pretty good, don't you agree?

My brother Finn's boycott has been as long and almost as successful.

Even Mum and Dad are using the car less, they both said so. They haven't officially joined my boycott, but they can't drive around so much if me and Finn won't get in the car.

Mum suggested I should celebrate my four-week anniversary by baking a cake, but instead I've been writing messages to the school governors and the local council.

I wrote pretty much the same letter to all of them. Dad said they wouldn't mind.

'Don't waste your time writing it again and again,' he said. 'Just copy and paste the text.'

Dad suggested I should write to our local MP too. I said our MP isn't going to be very interested in my ideas because MPs don't care about anyone under the age of eighteen. We can't vote for them.

Dad said I was wrong. 'An MP is supposed to represent the views of all their constituents, even the ones who can't vote. If you're not happy about the pollution in your local area, they have

121

to do something about it, or at least give a response. That's their job.'

Dad helped me find my MP's email address. Now I've written to her. I hope she writes back soon, although Dad says I will probably have to wait a month for a reply, if not two. Apparently politicians are very busy.

 **FIND YOUR LOCAL MP**

UK Parliament

House of Commons > MPs and Lords > Find MPs > Diana Jarvis

Your Member of Parliament is

Diana Jarvis

| ABOUT |
| CAREER |
| CONSTITUENCY |
| VOTING HISTORY |
| FAQs |
| CONTACT |

> Diana has lived in the constituency for seven years. Before she was elected to parliament, Diana worked as a solicitor. In her spare time, Diana enjoys baking and hill-walking. She has two children.

FROM Hope Jones
TO Diana Jarvis MP
DATE Wednesday 2 July
SUBJECT Protecting my primary school from cars

Dear Diana Jarvis,

I am at Durdle Primary School and I have a question for you: will you protect me and my fellow pupils from cars?

If you're wondering why I'm so worried about cars, the answer is very simple: cars are killing us!

Here are some small changes that would make a big difference to our school.

1: Install air filters in every classroom.

2: Plant a green wall around the playground, full of plants which will soak up pollution, and stop us from being poisoned by all the cars and lorries in the streets around the school.

3: Pedestrianise the streets immediately around the school. Parents and staff have to walk or cycle to school. No cars!

Unfortunately these changes are expensive, but could you help to get some money to pay for them?

I can't vote for you now because I am not old enough to vote. But if you make these changes to my school to stop pollution and save us from cars, I promise I will vote for you as soon as I'm eighteen.

Yours sincerely,
Hope Jones
(Ten years old)

THURSDAY 3 JULY

I told my whole class about Amsterdam. Miss Brockenhurst asked me to bring in some pictures to show to everyone. I described Anne Frank's house, the Van Gogh museum, those delicious Dutch waffles – and, of course, I told them all about Zoe's neighbourhood.

'I wish I lived there,' Clem said.

Me too!

I described the changes that I want to make around here and explained how I had been inspired by Zoe's street and neighbourhood. I told them what I had suggested to Mr Khan and I described my three big ideas.

To my surprise, everyone thinks they're great – even Tom and Aaron.

'I love cars,' Tom explained. 'But I don't need to drive to school in one.'

There's only one problem: everyone might agree with my ideas, but no one knows how to make them happen. Somehow we have to persuade our parents, the school governors and the local council to take us seriously and change things round here.

'I know what the problem is,' Harry said. 'Adults don't care. They're never going to care because they're only worried about their own little problems.'

He reminded me of what Mrs Ahmed had said about adults barely having enough time or space in their brains to worry about their mortgages and what to cook for tea, so not having anything left over for things like pollution or the future of our species.

Harry was very philosophical about it all. He said, 'We'll probably be just the same when we're older too. That's why we need to save the world now, while we're still young, and we've got the time and energy to do something about it. As soon as we're old enough to have our own jobs and mortgages, we won't be interested anymore because we'll be worrying about them instead.'

Miss Brockenhurst didn't agree with Harry. 'Adults *do* care, but we feel just as helpless as you,' she said. 'We don't know what to do either. I'd much rather live in a lovely clean street like Zoe's. I hate breathing polluted air, but I don't know how to make things better.'

Maybe Miss Brockenhurst and Harry are both right. Maybe some adults care about other people and want to make the world a better place, but just don't know what to do, but other adults simply don't care about anything except themselves, which is why they sit in their cars with the engines running, pumping pollution into the air.

🚲 Hope Jones' Blog 🚲

FRIDAY 4 JULY

Dad was wrong! I didn't have to wait a month for Diana Jarvis MP to reply, let alone two. She has replied to me already.

FROM Diana Jarvis MP

TO Hope Jones
DATE Friday 4 July
SUBJECT Re: Protecting my primary school from cars

Dear Hope,

Thank you for your message about your school.

I agree that pollution and climate change are two of the most important issues facing humanity and our government at this time.

If you check my record, you will see that I have asked three questions in the House of Commons about pollution-related issues and eleven more about climate change.

Please rest assured that I will do everything in my power to mitigate the impact of pollution and climate change on my constituents.

Thank you again for your correspondence. If you have any future queries or concerns on this issue or any other, please do not hesitate to contact my office.

Yours sincerely,
Diana

Diana Jarvis MP
House of Commons
London
SW1A 0AA

There's just one problem.

In my letter, I had begged for her help with pollution and asked if she could make three specific changes to our school, but she didn't even answer that part of my letter. In fact, she didn't say very much at all.

I showed the letter to Dad. He said, 'Politicians! They're all the same.'

He should know. He works in local government.

He said, 'They talk and they talk and they talk, but they never actually say anything.'

Just like Diana Jarvis!

She has written a whole email to me, full of words, but she doesn't actually say anything.

🚲 Hope Jones' Blog 🚲

SATURDAY 5 JULY

Life is full of surprises.

Today, for instance, I had a very surprising conversation with Mr Crabbe.

I told him about my weekend in Amsterdam and how I would like to change our neighbourhood. I showed him the before and after pictures of Zoe's street.

Imagine if our street was as beautiful and clean as Zoe's, I said to him. Imagine if the road was ripped up and replaced with a lawn and trees and cycle paths. Imagine if flowers grew outside every house. Imagine if cars couldn't drive down this street, and the air was fresh and clean, and no one coughed or choked from the poisonous pollution. Imagine if we could breathe.

To my amazement, Mr Crabbe liked the sound of that.

'It would be a big improvement,' he said. 'When I was a kid, there weren't so many cars around. We could play football up and down the street.'

129

He had such a sad smile, I thought he might actually join my boycott.

'There's just one problem with your plan,' Mr Crabbe said. 'It's a beautiful fantasy, but we live in the real world.'

'What if we change the world?' I said.

'Good luck with that,' Mr Crabbe said.

I told him about my letter to Diana Jarvis MP and her reply.

'You can't trust politicians!' he said. 'They're only out for themselves.'

I think he might be right. I hope the school governors are different.

🚲 Hope Jones' Blog 🚲

SUNDAY 6 JULY

Granny and Grandad came to lunch today. I'm sorry to say that they drove here in their car.

'You should be pleased,' Grandad said. 'At least we only drove one car, we could have brought them both.'

Granny and Grandad still have two cars, but Granny has been trying to walk more. She's even got herself a fitness tracker.

'I've done *at least* ten thousand steps every day,' she said. 'I'm going to buy one for your grandfather too. He needs to take more exercise.'

'I play golf!' Grandad protested.

'Once a week. You ought to be exercising every day. Like me!'

They both wanted to hear about my trip to Amsterdam. I told them how I have been inspired to change things round here. To my surprise, they both thought my ideas were brilliant.

'I wish we could help,' Granny said. 'Is there anything we can do?'

'You could sell one of your cars,' I said, 'and buy bikes instead.'

'Now, now,' Grandad said, 'your grandmother didn't mean that. She meant how can we help with your school?'

Granny said, 'We could write to the head teacher. Surely he'd like to hear from your grandparents?'

That would be great! I gave Mr Khan's address to Granny and Grandad. I suggested that they could write to the school governors and the local council too.

'You shouldn't bother with the politicians,' Grandad said. 'They're all useless! If you want to get something done, you have to do it yourself.'

'I can't do any of these things,' I said.

'You could build a green wall,' Grandad said.

'I couldn't,' I said.

'Why not?'

'I don't know how.'

'You could find out,' Granny said. 'Look it up. I bet the internet is full of information.'

'I'll help you build it,' Grandad said. 'We both will.'

I was amazed. Would they really do that? Would they come to my school and build a green wall?

'Of course we will,' Grandad said.

'We'd love to,' Granny said.

Nothing makes them happier than a project.

Grandad grabbed some paper and a pen, then started writing a TO DO list. Granny searched on the internet for the best plants to protect people against pollution. By the time Dad called us for lunch, we had made a plan.

My granny and grandad are amazing!

'You could do our garden next,' Mum said. 'It needs some love and attention.'

Mum and Dad never have time for gardening. Dad says he'll start on the garden once us three kids have left home and he has a moment to himself.

'One thing at a time,' Grandad said. 'We'll build Hope's green wall first, then maybe we'll come and give you a hand here.'

Granny and Grandad have amazing plans for the green wall. I can't wait to see them turned into reality! I just have to hope the school lets me.

MONDAY 7 JULY

Today I talked to Mr Khan and told him about Granny and Grandad's idea. I was worried he might laugh at me or tell me not to be so silly, but he was actually really interested. He promised to help in whatever way he could.

I said, 'When could we build the wall?'

'When do you want to start?' he asked me.

'How about next weekend?'

Mr Khan laughed. 'You don't hang about, do you?'

I reminded him about Selma's asthma attacks. I never want to see her having another.

'Next weekend it is,' Mr Khan said.

I could hardly wait for the day to be over. I rushed out of school, borrowed Mum's phone, rang Granny and Grandad, and told them the good news.

Grandad had good news of his own. He had spent the day ringing round local garden centres, asking if any of them would donate some plants for our green wall. The first three said no, but the fourth said yes. Thank you, thank you, thank you, Pavel and Lucinda at the Blooming Marvellous Garden Centre! I can't wait to come and meet you this weekend.

Grandad said, 'Now we just need a small army to carry the plants, dig holes and do all the work.'

I told him not to worry. I know where to find an army.

❀ Hope Jones' Blog ❀

TUESDAY 8 JULY

Sometimes school can be very frustrating. I had so much to do today! I wanted to talk to people about my plans and invite them to come and build the green wall at the weekend, but Miss Brockenhurst told me that I could only have those conversations during my breaks because lesson time is for lessons.

'This is more important than lessons!' I told her.

'There'll be time for everything,' Miss Brockenhurst said. 'Come on, everyone. Places, please. Today we're going to be learning more about the Ancient Egyptians.'

I tried to concentrate on the building of the pyramids but I could only really think about building the green wall.

During break, I talked to as many people as possible, inviting them to come and help us on Sunday.

'Ask your parents,' I said to everyone. 'Bring your brothers and sisters, your grannies and grandpas, your uncles and aunts. We need as many people as possible.'

Harry said yes, definitely, he will be there. Gwen, Selma and Vivek will come too if their parents let them. Mr Khan promised to put a note in the newsletter. I hope everyone reads it! We need as many helpers as possible.

I found three more after school. Becca picked me up and took me to Flat White, where she was meeting Tariq and Sparkle.

Flat White is my favourite café in the entire world. Brendan is the owner and he makes the best hot chocolate that I have ever tasted. Today he gave me a free flapjack to dip in it. YUM.

We had a quick chat about pollution. Brendan and his girlfriend Leah are doing whatever they can to make Flat White more eco-friendly. They both cycle to work. Their coffee arrives in an electric van. Brendan transforms all the used coffee grounds into compost. He only sells cups which can be recycled. He got rid of the plastic spoons and replaced them with reusable metal ones.

If only every café in the world was like Flat White.

I told Tariq and Sparkle about my trip to Amsterdam, my discussions with Mr Khan, my letter to Diana Jarvis MP, and my plans for building the green wall, and I told them that I was worried not enough people would turn up on Sunday, leaving me, Granny and Grandad to dig a hundred holes and plant all the shrubs, flowers and bushes.

'I'll help,' Sparkle said.

'Me too,' Tariq said.

'Me three,' Becca said, which was great, because she hadn't actually offered to help at all till now.

'We could make a film while we're there,' Tariq said. He is going to message his friend Claude, who works for a news website and could make us go viral.

'I can help you make some banners or posters,' Becca said. 'We can print them out in the art department at my college.'

'One person can't change the world,' Sparkle reminded me. 'But if we join together, and make our voices heard, we can make a difference.'

She's right! I can't do anything alone. I'm just one small person. But if I work with my friends, my family and my neighbours, together we can change the world.

WEDNESDAY 9 JULY

Twenty-three more people have said they're coming to help at the weekend! Half my year will be there, and lots of other kids too, all bringing their parents.

I have heard from one person who definitely can't come. Zoe would have loved to nip over from Amsterdam, but couldn't find a cheap train ticket.

I said she should come later in the year when the green wall has had a chance to grow a bit.

'I would love that,' Zoe said.

Aunt Jess can't come either, but she's going to check my blog regularly for photos and updates.

We might even be in the local paper! Dad has been in touch with a couple of his contacts and invited them along. He also suggested I should write to our MP again. Apparently politicians are always interested in free publicity, particularly if it's a good news story.

FROM Hope Jones
TO Diana Jarvis MP
DATE Wednesday 9 July
SUBJECT Visiting my school

Dear Diana Jarvis,

I wrote to you last week about my school, Durdle Primary.

I am writing to you again because something amazing is happening next Sunday. My friends, their parents, the staff and I are going to build a green wall around the school, protecting us from the terrible pollution in the surrounding streets.

Would you like to come and watch?

If you would, please come to Durdle Primary School next Sunday morning (the 13th of July).

Yours sincerely,
Hope Jones

THURSDAY 10 JULY

Do you want to stop pollution?

Will you come and help to build the green wall?

If you're at Durdle Primary: see you there at 10am on Sunday!

If you're not at Durdle Primary, unfortunately you can't come, because Mr Khan says only pupils, parents and guardians will be allowed. Otherwise there would be safeguarding issues.

But here's an idea: why don't you build a green wall in your own school instead? You can protect the playground from pollution and save your lungs. And if there's anyone in your school like Selma who gets asthma, you'll be doing them a big favour too – they won't have to move away!

We can't all live on top of a mountain, or even in Amsterdam, but we could all have green walls around our schools.

Durdle Primary
newsletter

Week ending: Friday 11 July

It's been another wonderful week at Durdle, full of good learning and interesting experiences.

Congratulations to Ravens, who achieved a 99.2% attendance this week! Let's see which class will be the first to reach 100%!

Thank you to all the parents who attended our Special Assembly on Wednesday to explain our new Maths Challenge. It was wonderful to see so many of you there. Some of you do need to practise your times tables. No names – but you know who you are!!!

Finally, just a reminder that there is a very special event in the school on Sunday 13th July at 10am, when Hope in Otters is going to be leading a massive effort to build a green wall around the school, protecting us all from pollution. Please come along if you can – and don't forget to bring your own gardening equipment (Hope particularly recommends strong gloves and a trowel). Don't forget to bring some water too; the forecast is clear skies and glorious sunshine.

Have a lovely weekend.

Mr Khan

SATURDAY 12 JULY

I'm exhausted! I'm almost too tired to write anything. I've spent the whole day with Granny and Grandad, carrying plants around. You would have thought plants are light, being not much more than a stick and some leaves, but they are actually exceedingly heavy.

'You see?' Grandad said. 'Cars can be useful!'

I had to agree with him. There is literally no way we could have collected all those plants from the garden centre and carried them to the school, ready for planting tomorrow, without a car.

'But you don't need two,' I reminded them.

Granny and Grandad both smiled.

'We're actually thinking of cutting down,' Granny said.

'We're discussing it,' Grandad added quickly. 'We haven't made a decision yet.'

But I could see Granny had decided – even if Grandad hasn't.

I'm so proud of you, Granny and Grandad! Thank you for caring so much about the future and the planet!

I also want to say a huge THANK YOU to Pavel and Lucinda, who have been amazingly generous. They have donated hundreds of plants for our school – and given us an enormous discount on lots more.

If you need some bulbs, seeds, or any other gardening supplies, I can recommend the Blooming Marvellous Garden Centre. They're the best garden centre for miles around!

I have to go and lie down now.

Tomorrow is going to be a big day.

SUNDAY 13 JULY

When I woke up this morning, I felt terrified. What if no one came to school? What if I was all alone with three hundred plants and twenty bags of fertiliser? I'd look like such an idiot! Luckily I didn't have time to think any more bad thoughts, because Dad put his head round the door and told me to run downstairs for breakfast.

'We don't want to be late, do we?'

Something amazing was waiting for me at the kitchen table: my sister Becca. She's never got up for breakfast on a Sunday before. Soon I realised why: the doorbell rang, and her friends Tariq, Sparkle and Claude came round. They were all bleary-eyed and grumpy. I don't think they'd ever been up so early either.

After some breakfast and a lot of strong coffee (for the teenagers), we went into the garden, raided the shed, and armed ourselves with spades, forks, rakes, trowels and gloves, plus Dad's toolbox.

Then we went to school.

We weren't the first to arrive. Granny and Grandad were waiting outside the school – with a small crowd of kids and their parents who had got there before us. I apologised for being late and explained it was because of the teenagers, but no one minded.

Mr Khan was standing by the entrance with Dave the site manager, who had just opened the gates.

Lots of other teachers had come too.

Like Miss Brockenhurst, for instance, who brought her boyfriend Fabrice. (He's so French! And very handsome.)

More people arrived every minute. I couldn't believe how many people had given up their Sunday morning to help!

'We wouldn't have missed it for anything,' Selma's mum said.

Gwen came with her two elder brothers. Aaron brought his uncle, who is a professional gardener. Vivek had his dad with him; it turns out that he's an engineer and he has some great ideas about anti-pollution devices for the school and the playground. He's already arranged to meet one of the school governors to discuss how they might be able to work together. Thank you, Mr Sidhu!

Harry brought his Baba and Jiji, who are visiting from Japan. (Baba and Jiji is what you call your granny and grandpa if you're Japanese.)

Of course, there were lots of people who couldn't come, because they were busy with other things. Like JJ, for instance, who has Korean school on Sunday mornings, and Lilly and Oliver, who have football, and Hassan, who was visiting his auntie in hospital.

Actually it's lucky that not everyone could come, because the playground was packed with people. Any more and we would have been overwhelmed. That's what Mr Khan said, anyway.

'I wish we could get a crowd like this for Meet the Teacher,' he said. Then he looked at me. 'So, where shall we start?'

That was when it struck me. I was responsible for bringing all these people together. They had come to school rather than playing football or lazing around in bed or doing whatever they usually chose to do on an ordinary Sunday morning. Now I had to tell them what to do next. If everything went wrong, it would be my fault. I was in charge!

Luckily I had Mum to help me. She's brilliant at organising. I think I must have inherited it from her. Together we divided everyone into groups and gave them different tasks.

Some people started digging holes in the soil. They were helped by kids who cleared away stones and pebbles.

Others divided up the bushes and vines from the garden centre, then carried them to different parts of the playground.

Until this week, I didn't really know anything about gardening, but I have learned one very important thing. If plants are going to grow up to be big and strong, they need a lot of love, a lot of affection, and a lot of chicken poo, so another team opened bags of fertiliser and poured precisely the right amount into each hole.

Being in charge was a big responsibility. I wanted to work as hard as anyone else – if not harder, to show them how much I appreciated their efforts.

I would have been happy to dig and plant and fertilise and organise non-stop, but I did have to take a break in the middle of the morning so I could talk to Diana Jarvis MP.

That's right! My Member of Parliament actually came to our school. To meet me!

'I'm sorry I didn't reply to your message,' she said. 'But I'm very pleased that I could come and meet you instead.'

Diana Jarvis might sound quite boring in her emails, but she's actually really nice when you meet her. I don't know why everyone complains about politicians all the time. As far as I could see, they're just ordinary people doing their jobs like anyone else. I have only met one, and maybe the rest of the politicians are completely different, but I really liked Diana Jarvis. I'm glad she's representing us in Parliament.

She told me how much she cares about climate change.

She has two children who are very worried about the future of the planet, and are always asking her to change things.

'They want to know why the government can't work faster,' she said.

'I'd like to know that too,' I said.

'Big changes do take time,' Diana Jarvis said. 'We all have to be patient.'

'Climate change is happening right now!' I said. 'We don't have time to be patient!'

I told her how slowly things change at Durdle Primary.

It turned out that Diana Jarvis had already talked to Mr Khan. They had even discussed my proposals for changes to the school.

'Are you going to do them?' I asked.

'That's up to Mr Khan and the governors,' Diana Jarvis said. 'But I'll be very happy to lend my support and provide any assistance that the government can offer.'

All the teachers wanted to meet Diana Jarvis. Everyone shook hands and took photos.

Diana Jarvis had to rush off to another meeting. I hope she will do what she promised and implement all the anti-pollution measures that I have requested.

I asked Dad if he believed her. 'You said politicians lie all the time.'

'They tell the truth sometimes,' Dad said. 'Sometimes they even keep their promises. We'll just have to wait and see.'

We carried on working all day, only stopping for a quick lunch. Everyone had brought their own. The sun was shining. It was a beautiful afternoon. We would all have been happy to lounge about for hours, chatting or playing games, but I knew we had to keep going or we wouldn't finish by the end of the day. I stood up and clapped my hands.

'Come on, everyone!' I called out. 'Back to work!'

No one complained. Without moaning or groaning, they all sprang to their feet and started working again. It was amazing. They must have been exhausted – gardening is surprisingly tiring – but no one wanted another moment's rest.

I want to say one thing to everyone who came to Durdle Primary today:

THANK YOU!

Thank you for giving up your Sunday in exchange for nothing more than the satisfaction of helping your local community. And a free cup of tea, of course. Not to mention some delicious homemade flapjacks.

Mr and Mrs Papagiannis wanted to bring the tea and flapjacks to say thank you too.

'We're so grateful,' they said to me. 'We know you were inspired to do this because of Selma.'

'It's because I want her to stay round here,' I said. 'I don't want her to leave.'

'We know,' said Mrs Papagiannis.

They still haven't made any definite plans. They might even think again. If we can persuade the school and the local council to make some big changes to the local area and improve the air quality so people don't get such terrible asthma, maybe Selma will stay round here.

I hope so!

We had a break for drinks and flapjacks, then another break for lunch, and a third break for more drinks and more flapjacks, but we spent all the rest of our time working: digging holes, emptying bags of chicken poo, lifting plants from their pots and putting them in the ground, shovelling the soil back into place, and making everything look beautiful. It was exhausting!

By the end of the day, I could hardly move because my muscles ached so much. My hands were covered in dirt, and my clothes too, and I had cut my finger on a sharp stone, but I didn't care about any of that. I didn't even notice, because I felt such an amazing sense of achievement. We all did.

Together we had built a green wall around the school.

MONDAY 14 JULY

When I woke up this morning, I could hardly believe what we had all achieved together yesterday. It felt like a dream. I had to remind myself it really happened – we built a green wall around Durdle Primary!

I have to admit it's not a perfect solution. The streets around the school are still full of cars and lorries. But from now on, the air we breathe in our playground is going to be a little less polluted. It's a really good start.

I still want the school to install air filters in every classroom and pedestrianise the streets around the school, which is why Finn and I went back on our protest this morning.

Most people were much friendlier. They know more about pollution now – and they know they don't like it.

I asked Mr Khan how he got to school. He confessed that he had come by car again.

'But you've definitely inspired me with your wonderful work at the weekend,' he said. 'I'm not going to drive every day. I'll catch the bus as often as possible.'

'How about tomorrow?' I asked.

Mr Khan nodded. 'You're right, I should start as soon as possible,' he said. 'I'll come to school by bus tomorrow.'

That will be one less person using their car!

Becca came to the protest after school. So did Tariq, Sparkle, Sofia and several of their friends. Having so many people was brilliant.

We must have talked to fifty drivers, and almost all of them were friendly. Only one wasn't: a van driver who was making a delivery and wanted to take a short cut past our school. He stopped his van right in front of me and beeped his horn so loudly I thought my ears might burst.

'We're asking people to drive a different route at school drop-offs and pick-ups,' I explained to him. 'We don't want anyone polluting the air around our school.'

'I don't care about you or your school,' the driver said. 'I just want to make my deliveries on time.'

Then he beeped his horn once more and drove off.

tariq

535 likes

tariq Whose side are you on? It's time to make a choice. **#stopdriving #stoppolluting #nofossilfuels #walkdontdrive #bikedontdrive #savetheplanet #girlpower #hopejonessavestheworld**

TUESDAY 15 JULY

The green wall looks even better today. The plants must like their new home. Granny and Grandad said they'll take a few weeks to settle in and dig their roots deeper into the soil, but I think they're looking happier already.

This morning, Mum had a meeting first thing, so Becca walked me and Finn to school. When we got to Durdle Primary, we stood outside the school gates and talked to anyone who was coming past in a car. We told them that we want to keep the air clean for all the kids who were walking rather than driving.

So many people have already given up their cars! They've been inspired by the green wall.

Miss Brockenhurst cycled to school.

Mr Braithwaite ran all the way!

The teachers have a staff car park at the back of the school. Usually it's full, but today there were only nine cars. Maybe tomorrow there won't be any.

Even Mr Khan came to school on the bus.

'Every little helps,' he said again.

161

☙ Hope Jones' Blog ☙

Sometimes I get depressed. I feel gloomy because so many people don't seem to care about the future or the environment. Then I remind myself that most people are kind, generous and thoughtful – and most people *do* care about the future of our planet.

Like all the people who turned off their idling engines, for instance. And everyone who gave up their time to build the green wall on Sunday. And Pavel and Lucinda from the Blooming Marvellous Garden Centre, who gave us so many plants.

I've also been amazed by the kindness and generosity of people who I don't even know and haven't even met. Like Elizabeth, for instance, who reads my blog (hello, Elizabeth!) and sent me a present for our school playground – an air pollution monitor. We can just take a quick look at the dial and we'll be able to check the pollution levels – and see if it's safe to run around outside.

Thank you, Elizabeth!

We did our protest before and after school again today. There were more people walking than ever. They've all heard about pollution now. They know about the green wall too. And they all agree with me: we've got to clean the air because we need to be able to breathe.

Even Jemima Higginbotham has been inspired. She asked her dad to drop her at the end of the street, rather than right outside the school, and she walked from there.

'Maybe tomorrow you could walk all the way from home,' I suggested.

'Unfortunately that won't be possible,' Jemima said.

'Why not?'

'My dad has to drive straight to work after dropping me off,' she said. 'He couldn't walk here, then walk home and pick up his car, and then drive to work.'

'Why doesn't he get the bus?' I asked.

'Dad doesn't travel on buses,' Jemima said. 'He says they're only for poor people.'

Maybe Mr Higginbotham hasn't been convinced by my arguments, but lots of other people have. Like Miss Brockenhurst, for instance, who cycled to school again today, despite the weather. She usually drives on rainy days, but she's just bought herself a new waterproof jacket and waterproof trousers, so she's prepared for anything.

The teachers' car park only had seven cars today. Maybe tomorrow it will be down to zero!

Even Anthony has joined in. His big lorry was parked outside our school, delivering food for the kitchens, just as always, but one thing had changed. Anthony had turned off the engine – without us even needing to ask this time.

'Morning!' he shouted. 'Lovely day!'

'It is!' I called back. 'You know what would make it even lovelier? If you swapped your lorry for an electric one.'

'We're working on it,' Anthony said.

Apparently his boss has been researching models and costs. They're planning to transfer the whole fleet to electric as soon as possible.

The world is getting better! One lorry at a time.

Hope Jones' Blog

THURSDAY 17 JULY

Even more people walked to school today!

Pupils, parents and teachers.

There were only five cars in the staff car park. I don't think we'll ever get to zero: Mrs Baptist explained that she has to drop her niece at nursery on the way to work, which simply isn't possible on public transport, and Mrs Cohen has started doing a car share with three other teachers, so her car is practically a bus! But the car park was full a week ago, so having only five is amazing.

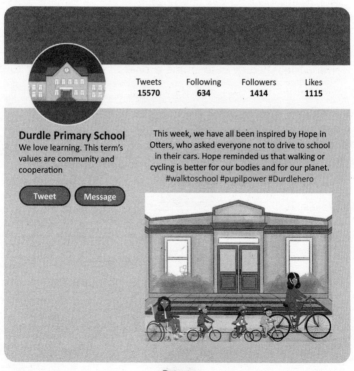

Tweets	Following	Followers	Likes
15570	634	1414	1115

Durdle Primary School
We love learning. This term's values are community and cooperation

Tweet Message

This week, we have all been inspired by Hope in Otters, who asked everyone not to drive to school in their cars. Hope reminded us that walking or cycling is better for our bodies and for our planet.
#walktoschool #pupilpower #Durdlehero

Mr Khan talked to me during break. Last night the school governors had their meeting. He told them all about me! He described my trip to Amsterdam, my protest and the building of the green wall.

'They all came outside to see what you'd done in the playground,' he said. 'They were very impressed. And inspired! They had so many questions. I should have asked you to come and talk to them.'

'Why didn't you?' I asked.

'Maybe next time.'

Mr Khan told me that the school governors want to get involved. They've agreed to divert a portion of the budget to environmental measures, and they're going to draw up a plan over the summer holidays.

'So they'll put air filters in the classrooms? And speak to the council about pedestrianising the streets?'

'Let's hope so,' Mr Khan said.

I was feeling so pleased with myself! But I felt even better when I got home.

Look!

Mr Crabbe hasn't given up his car, because he loves it too much, and he's still planning to drive to work most days. But he's bought himself a bike.

'It's not for the environment,' he wanted me to know. 'It's for my own health. My doctor advised me to buy this. He said I have to take more exercise.'

'That's great,' I said.

Mr Crabbe can get healthy while saving the world. Then everyone will be happy.

I told him about the green wall. 'We could do something like that in our street,' I suggested. 'We could grow plants and swap the parking spaces for cycle racks. Then the air would be clean and kids could play football in the street, just like when you were growing up.'

Mr Crabbe didn't say yes – but he didn't say no either. And he had a smile on his face when he rode away on his new bike.

FRIDAY 18 JULY

We're really making a difference.

Finn and I didn't bother protesting this morning, because there was basically nothing to protest against. A few parents dropped off their kids in their cars, but everyone else walked, cycled, or took public transport.

There were only two cars in the staff car park: one was Mrs Cohen's 'bus' and the other belongs to Mrs Baptist, who has to drive because of dropping off her little niece on the way to work.

Mr Khan came on the bus. Miss Brockenhurst biked. Even Dave, the site manager, who travels from miles away, took two buses and a train (you're a hero, Dave!)

Usually the air stinks around our school, but today was different.

Selma could take deep breaths without worrying about her asthma.

It was amazing!

Thanks for reading my blog. I hope you want to save the world too. Here are ten easy ways that you can join the fight against air pollution. Good luck! Love from Hope.

1. Stop driving! I know many people need to use a vehicle, but driving less will help the environment. Get on your bike instead! Go for a walk! Ride your scooter, your skates, or your horse!

2. If you and your family need to drive, then please try to drive efficiently and sensibly. For instance, you could make sure that your car's tyres are pumped up correctly. And how about sharing your car?

3. Use public transport. Buses, trams and trains are usually more efficient than cars, producing less pollution per passenger.

4. Write a letter to your local council or your MP, asking them to improve your local area for walkers and cyclists. We need safe streets!

5. Have you heard of Hydra? If not, why not look it up on the internet? It is a Greek island which has no cars. One day I'm going to visit Hydra, but for now, I just feel very inspired when I look at pictures of that beautiful island. All our villages, towns and cities should be designed around the needs of people, not cars.

6. Talk to your family, friends and neighbours. Do they know about the dangers of pollution? Could they walk or cycle rather than driving?

7. I'm sure you don't smoke. I hope you don't know anyone who does. But if you do: persuade them to stop! They will be healthier and the air will be cleaner.

8. Can you make any changes at your school? If you live in a town or city, can you persuade your school to build a green wall around the playground? Or plant a tree in the playground? Or grow some flowers or vegetables? How about closing the streets around the school during drop-off and pick-up, so everyone can walk or cycle safely?

9. Grow some plants at home. A few flowers, herbs, or vegetables won't make a big difference to air pollution, but they will improve your life in other ways: they will look nice, smell good and taste delicious.

10. Go outside. Wander through a park, a field, or a forest. Climb a hill. Our planet is beautiful. Remember why we care about it. Remember what we are fighting for.